I0594303

The University of Sydney, the chemistry building, the Carslaw building and so on are all real. However, the characters and events in this novel are not real, nor are they based on real people or events. And while I am sure that office politics can get to the point where people feel like killing each other, I think it is a very rare event that this actually happens and I know that murder is never a good idea.

Deadly

Miscalculation

R. J. Amos

1

While Nate lifted my heavy black suitcase into the back of his car, Jan stood on the footpath of Hobart airport and enveloped me in a huge hug. It was so good to see them again. I wanted to leave all the madness of the past two weeks behind. Sydney felt like another world, the flight home like closing the cover of a nightmarish book. Applying for a job wasn't supposed to be this complicated.

But of course I couldn't leave it behind. As I settled in to the back of the car and fastened my seatbelt, Nate turned around from the driver's seat to look at me reprovingly.

'Tell me, just how did you get yourself mixed up in yet another murder?'

'Oh Nate,' Jan intervened. 'It wasn't her fault. I'm sure.'

I thought about that for a bit.

'I'm not sure that it wasn't my fault. Maybe if I hadn't been there it wouldn't have happened.'

Nate pulled the car out from the kerb.

'See?' he said to Jan. 'She's making it happen now. It's like those firies who set the fires themselves so that they can put them out and be the heroes.'

'Alicia's not like that.' Then Jan twisted around to look at me over her shoulder. 'You're not, I know it.

I mean, you didn't actually do the murder, did you?'

'Jan!' I was hurt. 'You have to ask that?'

'You see?' she said to Nate. 'It's not her fault.'

'So what makes you think you brought it about then?'

I hesitated, then blurted out the thoughts that had been repeating in my brain like a broken record. 'If I hadn't had that coffee with her, if I hadn't showed that I cared … if I had just kept the status quo, then maybe she wouldn't have died.'

Jan reached back and patted my knee.

'Maybe you need to tell us the whole story.'

'Oh …' I hesitated. I didn't want to bore them. I wasn't sure I wanted to go through it myself.

'Come on Alicia, we're dying to hear. And we have the whole car trip home, and then you are going to join us for dinner. You knew that, didn't you?'

I didn't know, but I had guessed that Jan would be gracious and cook a meal for me. She's like that. She is the most hospitable person I know.

'So spill!' Nate was a little more forceful.

'Where do I start?' This wasn't a story that you could begin in the middle.

'How about why you chose to go for that job in Sydney rather than staying here with us.' Jan made it sound like I'd done something to insult them.

'So right at the very beginning, then?'

'It's always a good idea.'

I looked out the window at the beautiful green fields, the hills, and the glimpse of the mountain that guarded Tasmania's little capital city. The sight of that mountain always told me I was home. Always lifted my spirits.

Where was the beginning? The true beginning of this story was a few years ago when Mum rang me and was finally honest with me about just how sick she was.

2

I was working at the University of Sydney when that phone call came. It was dreadful, it made me feel sick to my stomach. It was the wakeup call that I really needed.

Finally, and much too late, I figured out that family is more important than a career; that I should have spent more time with Mum while I could; that I'd really put the wrong things first. I couldn't make up for the past, but I could spend every remaining moment with Mum. There was no hesitation. I left all my work unfinished and I really didn't care what kind of a mess I was leaving behind. I just told them I wasn't coming in anymore, and took the first possible flight to be where I belonged.

I spent those final months focusing on Mum. And after Mum passed away, I found I wasn't able to go back to work at the uni again. I wasn't able to do anything much for a while. And once I did find myself able to work, I figured that the 'academic career' part of my life was closed for good. You can't just step away from an academic job for a couple of years and then pick up where you left it. You have to keep the momentum going. Keep publishing, keep climbing the ladder. If you step away, you step away for good. At least, that's what I had been told.

It had taken me some time to pull myself together. But eventually I started thinking about work again. Wondering what I'd do with my life now. I tried to find work in Hobart, but there was nothing going except for a bit of casual work as a lab technician. It wasn't research, but it was better than nothing.

I was still in touch with Sydney University. Still receiving emails at my old address. And somehow, still on the mailing lists. And that's how I found that a position at my old stomping ground was open. There I was, wondering what I wanted to do, what options were available to me, and then this email. The position was lecturing and research, in my area, right there in my old department.

It was too good an opportunity to pass up. I had to go for it. Just in case there was the smallest chance that I could get it. I applied, and was shortlisted. It was miraculous. I had to go up to Sydney for the interview and to give a seminar.

And that's when I started to think again about the mess I had left behind before. I had been in the final stages of writing a paper and I had just stopped. I was sure that Professor Geoffrey Gray (or Prof Gray, as he preferred to be called), my old boss, hadn't been particularly happy with how I'd left things, though he was all kindness and consideration at the time. Would he support me in this application or had I burned my bridges?

I realised that the best way to approach this whole situation was to go to Sydney a couple of weeks before my interview. I was sure that the physical mess I'd left behind had been tidied away, but I could probably finish off the lab work and the paper that I had summarily dropped. It would get me back in the zone, give me something to say in my seminar and interview, and if I got the work to the point where a paper could be published, well, that would make sure that Prof Gray was properly on my side when the time came to make a decision about who to employ. His name would be on the paper as co-author, and another paper was always a good thing.

I wrote to Prof Gray and he said he was happy to have me in the lab group for a couple of weeks. And there it was, all falling into place. I was heading to Sydney for a couple of weeks, to work, write, and then give a seminar and be grilled in an interview. I was alternately thrilled and terrified. But determined to give this my best shot.

So I packed a suitcase, and caught a plane to the shiny city of Sydney. I decided to save money and instead of a taxi I caught a train to the closest station, then walked to the university. It didn't take too long to regret that decision – Sydney was a lot warmer than Tasmania and my clothing choice was far too warm for that kind of exercise. The suitcase was bulky and heavy and caught on tree roots, not to mention getting in the way of the other pedestrians.

It took all of my attention to keep it in line.

But as I walked the avenue to the chemistry building, the present faded and a lump in my throat grew as I relived old memories. The memory of my mother was so strong, the grief threatened to completely consume me.

I stood outside the front door, the hedges either side of the front steps giving a grand entrance feel. I was in a daze. Lost in old memories. I must have stood stock still for five minutes and I don't know how long I would have stayed staring at the door. Suddenly I was jolted back to the present by the force of someone tripping over my suitcase, ripping it out of my hand. A tall guy with a shock of black hair caught himself before he hit the ground, swore quietly (though, to be fair, not at me) and kept going, taking the steps two at a time. I yelled out, 'Hey!' but he didn't look back at all. Even as he raced up the stairs he was reading the print outs he was carrying – A4 pages covered with dense type – as if I didn't exist except as an unexpected obstacle in his road.

I was a little offended and my hand was more than a little sore. If I'd been a bit more alert I would have said something, but by the time I got a sentence together he had disappeared into the building. I picked up the suitcase again and checking around for more traffic, I lugged it up the steps and asked the receptionist for Prof Gray's office number, just in case it had changed.

It hadn't. And walking the familiar corridor, knocking on the door, and hearing his voice say, 'Come!' made me feel like I had stepped back in time. A lump rose in my throat. I almost expected to be able to go back to my old apartment, pick up my phone, and ring Mum. What I wouldn't give to be able to talk with her again. I hadn't expected this, the grief and the nostalgia. Well, I just had to move through it. I swallowed hard, composed what I hoped was a natural looking smile, and opened the door.

It was as if I had never left. Everything was exactly the same, down to the research posters hanging on the walls. Prof Gray looked up as I entered his office, a welcoming smile on his round cheerful face. He was a short, rotund man, with a ring of white hair around the bald spot on his head, and a little white goatee beard. He always reminded me of a gnome.

'Come in! Have a seat. Did you travel well?' He stayed seated at his desk not waiting for a reply to his questions. 'Just give me a minute, I'll just finish this email and then we can have a chat.'

In the centre of his office was a small, round coffee table surrounded by Swedish modern easy chairs. I sat down, trying to sit on the edge and look alert, but the chair pushed me back to a reclining position. So then I crossed my legs and tried to look relaxed. I was feeling neither alert, nor relaxed. My stomach was tense, and at the same time, a yawn was threatening to break through my control. I swallowed the yawn and looked around the office.

On the bookshelves with the textbooks and rows of journals were photos of Prof Gray. There was a very old one, in the faded colours of the seventies, of a group of about ten young, fresh-faced academics. There was Prof Gray at the beginning of his journey, already balding, but his hair still had some colour. There weren't many photos showing him before he looked as he did now. Was this what academic life did? Prematurely aged you? I looked for some photos of women to see what I was heading towards, but there were very few women to be found in the photographs around that office. There was one woman I could see, in that photo of a group of ten or so researchers. She had straggly hair, and could not be said to be wearing stylish clothes. But then, there I was in my jeans and t-shirt. I wasn't the most stylish person either.

I decided to stop making judgements. I looked at the trophies instead. And Prof Gray had quite a few of those. Medals and awards named after famous people. Maybe one day, if I worked hard, I could win one of those too. That's what I had been aiming for before. And I was about to jump right back into it.

Prof Gray finished his email and came and sat with me.

'It's good to have you back, Alicia.'

'Thanks for taking me on.'

'You made me an offer I couldn't refuse. To get that paper out would be great. I wasn't sure if you were coming back or not, so I didn't give it to another student. Then when it looked like you weren't coming back at all, I tried to get it finished. But to be honest, there hasn't been a student in the last year who has been interested in that side of the project. So it will be great to tie it up.'

'I'll do my best to put a neat bow around it.'

We chatted about legal requirements, about the paperwork I'd need to complete to be able to work in the university, and a little about the project. Reminding each other of where we were up to and what still needed to be completed.

Then Prof Gray slapped his hands on his knees and stood up.

'No time to lose, hey?' he said. 'Let's go and meet the group and get you set up in the office. I've organised that group meeting for you so that you can see what we're all up to now.'

I had asked for the group meeting. I had thought that starting the visit with an update on the research of the group would be a good idea, and Prof Gray had agreed with me. I was really looking forward to it. Just a few minutes from each of the members of the research group on their own projects and progress. It would propel me right back into the headspace I needed. At least I hoped it would.

Once more dragging my suitcase behind me, I

followed him through the corridors to the glass doors that fronted our group's laboratory.

3

Prof Gray swiped his card on the card reader at the door and indicated the safety glasses I should wear as we walked into the lab. The office was at the rear of the laboratory, but to get to it we had to walk past the liquid nitrogen dewars, the instrument that took surface area measurements of porous solids, the sinks with the glassware stacked precariously on the draining boards, and the ovens – muffler ovens for calcining at near a thousand degrees, drying ovens at 100°C and the more delicate drying ovens at around 80°C. That was all on our left, and on our right were the banks of fume hoods, stretching from floor to ceiling. The fume hoods (12 in total) enclosed the benches where the researchers actually did their chemical reactions. The fans in the hoods were constantly humming, pulling any dangerous fumes or vapours through to the scrubbers in the roof. Between that, the clicking of the instruments, and the radio constantly playing music, the lab was a noisy place.

At the end of the lab stood bright yellow floor-to-ceiling cupboards dividing the messy experimental space from the office space beyond. Unless something had changed since I had been here last (which was unlikely), the left-hand-side cupboards contained paperwork: material safety data sheets, risk analyses, and a copy of every thesis ever written by a group member. On the right were the chemicals, everything from acetic acid to zinc, but not in alphabetical order, that would be dangerous. I mean, storing acetic anhydride next to acetaldehyde is asking for a nasty explosion. And that's not the only thing that could go wrong. The chemicals were arranged according to dangerous goods code and hazard, acids together, metals together, and so on, so as to avoid a nasty incident or an explosion. And on the back side of the cupboard bank, the office side, there were consumables – disposable gloves, paper towel, that sort of thing.

I hauled my suitcase into the office and looking at the cramped cubicle space I could immediately see that something had changed. The only person I recognised was Robbie, the lab manager. All the students and post-docs who had been there only two years ago had gone, and new people had taken their place. It was to be expected; students finish their PhD studies and move on. Post-doc contracts are short, just one or two years. But still, it was a bit of a shock. I'd have to talk to Robbie about it later and find out what had happened to everyone.

Prof Gray introduced me to the new group.

'Everyone, this is Alicia. She's going to be doing a bit of work here over the next couple of weeks.'

There was a chorus of 'hi' and 'hello' from around the office.

'Nice of you to see fit to come back and join us,' Robbie said with a mock growl that made me feel more at home than the polite greetings from the others. I responded with airy disdain.

'No problem, I was just waiting for the invitation and then I was on my way.'

Prof Gray chuckled (for which I was grateful).

'Your desk is over here next to Rebekah's,' Robbie said. Then, he looked at the piles of paper, printed articles and student lab books that covered the desk and sarcastically commented, 'At least, you were intended to have this desk.'

'Oh, I forgot,' said the girl sitting at the desk one over from mine. She flicked her ratty brown hair over her shoulders, pushed up her sleeves, and started picking up pieces of paper at random from the piles. 'I'll have it ready for you in a tick.'

'Go ahead, but remember group meeting is in ten minutes. I'll leave you to settle in, Alicia. See you all soon.' With that, Prof Gray left.

Robbie again looked at the mess on what would be my desk, and then looked at me. 'Want to get a coffee while this is being sorted out?'

Did I ever! Coffee was a brilliant idea. But …

'Sounds good,' I said. 'Where should I leave my suitcase?'

There wasn't much space anywhere in the office. Each of the desks was a tiny cubicle, one row of five cubicles sat against the windows. There was just enough room behind the desks to allow a person to stand up and push their chair back before the chair would run into a bookshelf that divided the office in two length-wise. The other two rows of desks were set up against the back of the bookshelf, and up against the interior wall of the office. There wasn't any unused wall space, or even space under a desk to store something as large as my suitcase.

'That's a pretty big case.' The rude remark came from the back corner of the office. It was the same lanky guy who had tripped over me at the front door.

'Well, it has a few week's worth of clothes in it,' I retorted.

'I guess when I travel I just take a backpack.'

I wanted to ask whether he just wore the same clothes over and over, whether he cared about smelling fresh. I guessed I would work that out as the weeks went on. I took a breath and realised that I was reacting far too strongly. I grinned at Robbie and he rolled his eyes at me. I suddenly felt a great need to talk with him privately. I needed some background info about the people I'd be spending the next two weeks with.

'How about we put it here in front of the consumables cupboard for the time being?' he suggested. 'It won't get in the way too much, and besides, we're spending most of the afternoon in a group meeting now.'

'I know, all afternoon in group meeting.' This grumble came from the same lanky guy and was acknowledged by the other desks. It looked like I had put my foot in it before I even entered the room. I didn't think that my request for an update would be so difficult, but the moaning of the students implied that it was a huge ask. They didn't want to go to an extra group meeting, they had spent hours preparing the PowerPoint presentation, hours they didn't have. They could think of an infinite number of ways that they could have better spent the time.

It wasn't an auspicious start to my visit.

Suitcase safely stowed, Robbie and I left the others to their moaning and went for coffee. I started to walk back through the lab but Robbie said, 'Not that way, come here.' And opened the heavy door to the fire escape instead.

'It's just so much quicker to get out of the building this way,' he said as we walked down the two flights of stairs. 'No big corridor to walk along.'

'Oh, sure.'

I felt a bit slow, not remembering the fire escape. That's how we always used to leave the lab, especially when we were ducking out for a quick coffee. I needed to get back in the swing of things. What else had I forgotten that used to come naturally?

4

The closest café to the chemistry building faced it across the avenue. As we crossed the wide pedestrian thoroughfare we could see the line of patient customers through floor-to-ceiling windows. It looked like some things hadn't changed. They had always made a very decent coffee at that café but that meant long lines and a fair wait. Well, today that was good. I'd have time to have the chat I wanted, get the background info on the new team members and find out what had changed. I started by asking Robbie where all my old colleagues had gone.

'Yeah, pretty much the whole team has changed. Aaron and Pili graduated last year. Jen is doing a year with our German partners, and Dom got a permanent position with the enemy.'

'UNSW? How dare he?' I said in mock horror.

'Can't turn down permanency. I just wish I'd been able to get it. But yeah, you'll find there's hardly anyone in the team that you know.'

I shook my head.

'Weird, it doesn't feel like I've been away that long. In fact, it's already beginning to feel like I haven't been away at all.'

'It's good to have you here.' Robbie looked over his shoulder then continued in a conspiratorial mutter.

'I've been run off my feet teaching all these new people how to do the basics. I mean it's good for Prof's group to be growing but it would be better for me if he didn't leave all the training up to me.'

Training? Was I supposed to train the students? I hoped not.

'I'm not sure I'm going to be any help to you with that. I'm so out of practice. And I'm only here for a few weeks.'

Robbie slapped me on the back.

'Sure. No, I'm not expecting you to do anything like that. I'm just happy I don't have to train you. I'm sure that you will remember the lab protocols, and that you can still work the muffler furnaces. It would just be good if Mike pulled his weight, you know? He's "second in command", after all.' Robbie used his fingers to make the air quotes and I wondered which of the office-mates was Mike. 'But he leaves it up to me. What are you going to be doing, anyway?'

I breathed a sigh of relief.

'If you haven't thrown out my samples, I'm going to be finishing off the analysis so I can write them up. I have all the results of my experiments. I just need to do the surface area and the ICP and that stuff.'

'Just need to know what you actually made?' Robbie grinned.

'That's the one.'

When you're making a chemical compound you can put together a recipe, but the proof of the pudding, in this case, is in the analysis. BET analysis measures the surface area of the compound, ICP blasts it into smithereens and finds out exactly what elements are there, NMR looks at how they are connected. All sorts of instruments with three-letter acronyms (TLAs) used to describe them. And then, importantly, you also need to know whether whatever you made does what you want it to do. Whether it works as a catalyst, or reacts in the correct way.

I had already made my compounds and tested them, and I knew they did the job of catalysis that I wanted them to do. But before I could publish, I had to find out exactly what each compound was. And I would work that out, all being well, in the next two weeks, by performing various kinds of analysis.

I really hoped that Robbie had not thrown out my samples. I didn't have time to start from scratch, make everything again and repeat all the experiments I had already done. If there were no stored samples there would be no paper to write, no seminar to give (or at least, the seminar would be full of holes), and I would be wasting time. I was kicking myself for not checking this with Robbie before I came up. I mean, Prof Gray seemed to think that the samples would be there, but it was Robbie who really knew. I should have asked him.

Robbie clicked his fingers.

'I reckon I know where all your samples are. They'll be in a box in the cupboards under the fume hoods somewhere. First or second row, I reckon. Pili packed them up for you after you left so suddenly. Of course, it helps that you label everything. Not like some of these guys. Take Rebekah for instance, she has round bottomed flasks of goodness-knows-what and lines of sample tubes with black gunk in them at the back of her fume hood. You ask her to clean it up and she says "yes" and then does nothing. She's a hazard in the lab, if you ask me. And we have at least a year of her PhD to go, if not two, or four. It's not like she's going to finish on time.'

'Ah. Right.' I didn't really know how to reply to that.

I decided to focus on the good news. 'I'll remember to write to Pili and thank her for storing everything. I was such a wreck when I left, I know I couldn't have done it myself.'

'She was just happy to have your space in the fume hood. Remember? She was sharing with Dom and neither of them was happy about that.'

We were full into our chat then, reminiscing about days gone by. Our conversation naturally turned to the last time we had met. Robbie had come down to Hobart for a conference, a normal occurrence except for the murder of one of the keynote speakers at the conference dinner. We talked through just how I found the murderer and what had happened since.

'You'll be happy that nothing like that will happen in your visit here.'

'You know, Robbie, I don't want anyone to get killed anywhere.' I really wanted to make that clear.

'Sure, you enjoyed the notoriety. I know you. Alicia, the great chemistry detective.'

'Sure. Right. Whatever you reckon.' I punched him lightly in the arm.

'Now, now. Don't start with the violence. Seriously Alicia, are you trying to make something happen?'

I was grateful then that we made it to the top of the line and could order our coffees and break up the conversation.

'Who was the guy who was picking on my suitcase?' I asked as we stood in the next waiting area while the coffees were made, half listening for our names and half chatting some more.

'That's Mike. He's the guy I was telling you about. The 2 I.C. Or the biggest pain in the –'

' – in the group. Right. So it's not just me who thinks he's rude then?'

'No,' said Robbie flatly. 'I could do without him in the group to be honest. He's supposed to be helping out, but he's just making things worse as far as I can see. He only cares about himself and how fast he's climbing up the ladder.'

'That wouldn't make him any good at teaching the students.'

'Nope.'

'And why doesn't Prof Gray do anything about him?'

'Do what? He produces papers at the speed of light. Prof Gray thinks the sun shines out of his arse.'

I could understand what he was getting at. Papers were the currency of the academic world. I mean, that's one of the very big reasons that I'd invested in coming to Sydney. That, and getting my foot in the door for this new position. If you could produce loads of decent publications then I guess you could get away with being a pain.

The line had been longer than Robbie was expecting, but eventually, coffees in hand, we raced back up the stairs to the conference room, hoping to be there for the beginning of the group meeting.

5

'I hope the coffee was decent?' Jan asked as we climbed out of the car.

'Oh, it really was. That place makes a mean flat white. And it's funny, there is a little tent a bit further up the avenue that makes coffee too, but no one goes there unless they are in a desperate hurry. We all prefer the long line at the café.'

Standing in Jan and Nate's back yard I could hear the waves from the beach. Soon, soon I'd go for a long walk and let all the tension disappear into the waves. I might even do that tonight before bed. It was good to be home.

We walked up to the back door of Jan's café, in through the small hallway and Jan motioned that I should take a seat in one of her lovely red recliners.

'I'd prefer to stand actually. I've been sitting all day. Got some carrots you'd like me to peel or something to help with preparing dinner?'

Jan laughed. 'I'm sure I can find something for you to do. You too, Nate. Come on, we'll crowd into the kitchen and Alicia can keep telling us the story while we work.'

6

Despite the grumblings of the group, I was looking forward to the group meeting. I had been out of the loop for a couple of years, and hadn't heard much on the latest research. To be honest, I hadn't even read any research papers or tried to keep myself abreast of things. Somehow other things had seemed more important. Chatting with friends. Renovating my little cottage. Walking on the beach. That sort of thing.

Still, if I was a researcher (and on this trip I was going to try to convince the university that I was), then I needed to keep up with the research. I was hoping the students' three-minute talks would bring me up to date, or at least get my brain moving in the right direction.

I remembered a professor from my undergraduate days who told us all that he read the latest journal articles on a Saturday morning. How exotic that had sounded at the time. I was so sure that I'd be doing exactly the same thing. But pretty soon in my fledgling academic career I found that I wanted to spend my Saturday mornings in bed with a novel, not with more work, and that Saturday afternoons and Sundays had been spent catching up on the work I didn't manage through the week.

And now that I'd had a couple of years away from the hothouse I didn't think it was healthy to spend all weekend working. But maybe reading the latest research should be interesting, rather than work, I chided myself. Maybe if I was a true academic I would enjoy reading the latest research.

I sat between Robbie and Prof Gray and waited for the show to start.

Yusuf, a neatly dressed Malaysian student was the first up. His sage green business shirt was perfectly ironed, and he wore flashy cufflinks which had chemical symbols on them. He would have worn a tie, I'm sure, except that ties are not safe in the lab. His dark hair was held in a dapper quiff with large quantities of product. Everything about him said 'neat and tidy'.

He was working on some electrochemistry and his slides contained neat graphs with the cycling curves of oxidation and reduction. Yes, I remembered these, I couldn't really make out what it all meant, but then, he was only in the first year of his PhD and he probably wasn't sure what it all meant either. So many of us only figure out our PhD projects at the start of year three, trying and failing at so many different pathways in year one and two before we find the one that works. It makes for a stressful final year, but that's just the way it is.

Next up was Yumi, from Japan. Her laptop had a 'Hello Kitty' cover, and she wore a short tartan skirt with thick black stockings, and pink pompoms held her hair in pigtails. She unplugged Yusuf's computer from the projector, and plugged in her own. The display up on the wall went completely haywire – the slides were all pushed over to one side, the writing was squashed, we couldn't read a thing. Yumi pushed buttons and clicked her mouse, frowning at the computer screen. The display on the wall turned black, and then white, and then the squashed presentation showed again.

The students in the room started calling out advice.

'Unplug it and plug it back in.'

'Push F8.'

'Have you tried turning it off, and turning it back on again?'

In the end Mike and Yusuf could bear it no longer and got up to help.

The calls of advice petered out and we sat in uncomfortable silence, just waiting. Prof Gray did nothing to help; he just watched the panic with a small smile on his face.

Eventually he leaned over me to get Robbie's attention and said, 'This reminds me, I must get you to come and tell me how to put my unit outline up on the online learning. I can't figure out how to make it go.'

'I can come up after this,' said Robbie. 'If we ever get the projector working properly.'

'They're silly things,' Prof responded. 'If you can't give your lecture with a blackboard and chalk, then you probably don't know your stuff, if you ask me.'

I was wondering whether we would have to go to blackboard and chalk, or whiteboard and marker, or even sign language to hear Yumi's talk, when the wall filled with colour, she breathed a sigh of relief, and Mike and Yusuf sat back down so that we could begin again.

Yumi, as far as I could tell, was trying to break down the lignin of plants to make biofuel. However, it was difficult to understand much about her research as her shyness and quiet speech combined with her poor English meant I could only hear and comprehend one word in four. Her slides were impeccable – she must have spent ages on them – but her talking was nowhere near as confident. I felt sorry for her, worried that this stress of public speaking was too much for her. But as I looked around the room I could see that her faltering didn't bother the rest of the group. No one was shifting uncomfortably in their seat or blushing in sympathy like I was. They were all just relaxed and taking it in. This kind of talk was not an abnormal occurrence, apparently.

'Very good,' said Prof Gray when the whispers from the front slowed to a stop. 'Now we just need to get that into a paper. I want the rough draft on my desk by next week.'

Yumi gulped, nodded, and said, 'OK, yes. Next week, yes.' But it was obvious that she thought that was less than OK. I don't think she heard anything for the rest of the meeting, the pressure had been put on her, and she moved to the back of the room with her laptop so she could begin writing the paper while the rest of us continued to listen to the talks.

We moved on to Sofia, who was here in Sydney on a three-month exchange from Norway. She looked like a model – tall and slim with long blonde hair. And she dressed stylishly too, her long elegant scarf matched her grey eyes. My style, or lack of it – shirt, jeans, and sneakers – felt scruffy in comparison. Her talk was about catalysts that produced hydrogen for fuel cells. That was what the heading said. But mostly she told us about Norway, showing stunning pictures of fjords and mountains, and of course, the northern lights.

But if Sofia made me feel scruffy, the next presenter made me feel almost over-dressed. Wei from China, a short scrawny guy with a shaved head, wearing camouflage pants and a black T-shirt with holes in it. He gave me a smile as he started. The most friendliness I had experienced from any of the group members. He was an honours student, and his talk was all background to his project – he'd not had much of a chance to get started on the actual research yet – but the background for his project was also background for everyone else's, all the talks being in the same research area, and it gave me a wider understanding of the research the group was conducting. It was good practice for him, getting up and talking in front of everyone. And it was helpful for me.

Rebekah was next – her talk was as disorganised as the mess she had left on my desk, her accent strongly outback Australian. As she stuttered and stammered her way through I became aware of shared eye-rolls and meaningful looks between Mike, Wei and Sofia. It seemed there was a bit of bad blood in the group. Oh well, that happened. I wasn't going to get involved.

Then came Tony, also looking like he was from the outback, dressed in a checked shirt, moleskins, and boots. He gave a great talk, the best yet. Well prepared, a little bit of background and then his latest results. It looked like his research was going well, he had journal articles in preparation, and he was starting to talk about patenting at least one of his catalysts.

Sahar, from Iran, was working with plants to find biofuel. She also had a lot of work to show us. Too much for the three minutes – her talk went on for at least ten but despite our shuffling and Mike's finger tapping, she didn't give anyone the chance to interrupt, she just kept talking and talking. I became distracted by the amazing job she had done with her makeup. Beautiful dark eye makeup and bright red lipstick. She carried it so well. I dragged my attention back to the slides. There was good work here and I had asked to listen to it. I needed to focus.

The final speaker was Mike, and I could see what Robbie was saying about his work. He showed us enough results to fill three papers. It was a little intimidating. This was someone who would be difficult to compete with. I hoped I wasn't competing with him. Was he also going for the academic position? That would be a disaster. I might as well give up now.

As Mike finished talking about his final slide, Prof Gray sat up a bit straighter in his chair and put down the pen he had been making notes with.

'Thank you everybody. That was a good introduction to the group for Alicia. Make sure you make her feel welcome, won't you? Help her out in the lab if she needs it. Oh and speaking of the lab, Rob, any announcements to make?'

Robbie swivelled his chair round so that he was facing most of the group.

'Yep. A reminder about gloves. We're not using them, right? Not unless we really need them. You know how easy it is to get complacent when you're wearing them all the time. And you know Rebekah can't go near the latex ones, so nitrile unless you really have to use something else.'

Nods and choruses of, 'Yes Robbie,' went around the room.

'And whoever left that mess of white powder on the balance had better clean it up. I don't care what it was, none of us know and it could be anything. Balances need to be left clean and dry.'

'I agree with Rob,' said Prof Gray. 'Lab safety is no small thing. Make sure you keep the balances clean for your own safety and for the good of the instrument. No one needs a faulty balance.'

Then he stood and picked up his notebook and pen. Everyone else knew this was a symbol for us to leave, and with very little fuss or conversation the room emptied.

I followed close behind Robbie so that I had a way of getting into the lab and the office through the swipe-card-protected door. First thing tomorrow I would see the receptionist and try to get myself set up with my own swipe-card so that I didn't have to stick to someone's tail all the time, or interrupt someone working in the lab so they could let me in. I didn't want to be a pain.

7

I could see the surface of my desk in a few places when I got back into the office, but Rebekah was still working away at sorting the papers into piles and finding space for them on her already-crowded desk. So I decided the best thing I could do would be to remove myself and my suitcase and find out what my living quarters would be like for the next two weeks.

I had found a place that was reasonably cheap and also reasonably close to the university. It was called St Catherine's and had been recommended to me by a friend at church back in Tassie. The thing was, I didn't want to use up all of my savings by paying for accommodation so I was happy to find something so cheap. But I was also a bit nervous – how dirty and dilapidated was this place going to be?

Following the map on my phone, I walked down the avenue and turned right, then I walked up the street a few blocks until I found a little alleyway, pushed through a gate in a Colorbond fence and looked up to see a gracious mansion in front of me. A beautiful veranda was the first thing I saw, with grand columns, and wicker chairs spread around where you could relax and take in the semi-tropical garden, then behind the veranda rose the elegant old cream-coloured building, all three floors of it. I didn't notice until later the signs of extreme old age. The walls were in need of a coat of paint, some of the decking needed to be replaced, even the wicker chairs had a few holes half-hidden by lumpy cushions. But all this just added to the friendliness of the old building.

I dragged my suitcase up the driveway, the little wheels rattling over the pavers so loudly that I wondered that no one looked out any of the windows to see who was making all the noise. Then I lugged it up the wide front steps, across the veranda to the heavy wooden doors and entered into the quiet foyer. The faded red carpet and the dark wooden panelling made the house seem almost church-like. Everything was old, but it all felt clean and well looked after, which was a relief.

A steep staircase rose directly in front of me, the carpet almost worn through in the centre of the sloping treads. A little room off to the left looked like it might be a reception office, except for the fact that it was completely unattended. The hallway continued on past the staircase into a gloomy dusk. There were more doors, but they were all shut except for the office door and there were no signs or directions. I didn't know what to do. The place felt completely empty. Was I even in the right building?

I stepped into the little room on my left, and took a quick glance at the pamphlets laid out on a little table. They didn't help me. They seemed to be about training days and church activities and fundraisers for a local hospital. I looked over the higher counter that divided the room and saw a computer, and some filing cabinets. Beyond that was another door with an opaque glass window to what I presumed was a back-office, or inner sanctum where the work actually got done. Eventually I noticed a little bell on the counter next to a sign that said that I should ring for service. Peace filled the house like a warm blanket and I didn't really want to break the silence, but I was getting nowhere waiting for help to come. So reluctantly I rang the bell, the sharp tinkle piercing the calm. I almost wished I could take it back, un-tinkle the bell, bring back the quiet. But I had to find my room. I had to find out if I was even in the right place.

I waited for an age. Silence refilled the room and I started to wonder if I should ring the bell again, or go and try one of the closed doors. Eventually I heard the sound of a door opening and closing and an older woman appeared, not from the inner sanctum, but from the hallway. She was dressed in a pretty apricot shirt and blue slacks and she was wiping her hands on a floral apron. She looked slightly harassed, but had a friendly smile on her round and wrinkled face and her bright blue eyes sparkled.

'Hello dear,' she said. 'How can I help?'

'Is this St Catherine's?' I asked. 'I'm Alicia Conway. I'm here to check in.'

'Oh right. Yes.' She bustled past the counter and flipped over the pages of a large spiral-bound book that sat next to the computer. 'Right. Let me see. Elissa?'

'No. Al-ic-i-a, Alicia Conway.' I spoke more clearly and a bit more loudly in case she was deaf.

'Here for a while, are you dear?'

'Yes,' I said, increasingly concerned. 'Two weeks. Is that what you've got there?'

'Oh, I don't worry my head about those things. That's Sam's place to worry about. I'm just here looking after the place while he is off at the prayer meeting.'

'Right.' That was different. I'd never heard that while checking in to a hotel before.

'Here we go. I've got you. Room 221b, up on the second floor. Just like Sherlock, hey?' She grinned. 'Now, let me find the key.'

I sighed in relief. At least I had a bed for the night.

'Is there a lift?' I asked. I was so sick of hauling my case around.

She laughed, 'Oh no, dear. Just the stairs. Would you like me to help you?'

I shook my head. There was no way I was going to let that little old arthritis-ridden lady carry my suitcase. I pulled myself together for one last effort and followed my guide up the narrow wooden stairs, the suitcase balanced against my hip and bashing my ankle at regular intervals. I looked with interest

43

at the bookshelf on the landing (I'd have to come back and inspect that later) and then followed the woman along a narrow corridor until she stopped and pulled the key out of her apron pocket.

'Here we go. 221b. The toilet and shower are just down the hallway. And breakfast is served from seven until nine in the dining room, down on the ground floor. I'm sure you'll find it in the morning. Then there's a microwave and a fridge downstairs in the laundry if you want to store and cook your own food. Right, Luv?'

'Ah, thanks,' I said with very little enthusiasm. A shared bathroom? Was I really up for this? I knew the place was cheap, but I hadn't even thought about sharing a bathroom.

She opened the door and together we peered through into the bedroom.

'Oh no, I'm wrong.' She laughed at herself. 'Sam would have done a much better job settling you in. You're one of the lucky ones with an ensuite in your room. Well Luv, that's OK isn't it? Not having to traipse up the hallway to have your morning ablutions.'

Yes it was OK, it was very OK. I closed the door and sighed with relief listening to the stairs creak as she made her way back down to whatever I had interrupted. It felt good to be alone. I looked around at what would be my home for the next two weeks.

The little room had a double bed, one bedside

table, a wardrobe, and a wicker chair with a faded pink cushion. Everything clean but nothing luxurious. Everything old. An old faded print on the wall depicting vases of pastel pink flowers with a pastel blue background. Faded pastel pink and blue curtains. And an ensuite that had obviously been added in long after the original house was built.

It wasn't new and shiny but it was clean. This would be fine.

8

The next morning I opened my eyes when the alarm went off and lay in bed staring at the ceiling, feeling relaxed and happy. It almost felt like I was on holidays, and that didn't make any sense at all. I mean, I needed to get up and head off to work in the lab. I had a seminar to prepare, and a paper to write. I had to find all my samples and try and make sense of them. I had to figure out how to get writing done in an office where I wasn't even sure if I had desk space yet and I was pretty sure that my office mates hated me (or at least some of them did). But here I was, feeling almost like I did in the summer holidays as a kid.

Ah, that was the reason. It was warm. It felt like summer holidays.

It was September. At home the mornings were still bitterly cold. If it was a clear and sunny day then the frost was biting first thing, and if it was a cloudy day you knew you were in for horizontal sleet as you struggled in to work.

Here, by contrast, it was positively balmy, and I looked forward to the stroll down to the university. I wouldn't need my quilted jacket, I wouldn't need a beanie. I mean, it wasn't sandal weather by any stretch but it was still beautifully warm compared to the Tasmanian winter. And I didn't want sandal weather anyway. When you have to add a lab coat to your normal clothes and wear covered shoes, summer weather is just too hot.

My happy mood turned a little sour when I realised that I would have to get dressed and face people before my morning cup of coffee. Normally I'd make myself a cup and drink it in bed before facing any humans at all, but in this place that was not going to be possible. There was no kettle in the room and I would have to go down to the dining hall before I could eat or drink anything. That would mean I would need to be human before caffeine. I wasn't sure how possible that was, but I'd just have to give it my best shot.

I heaved myself out of bed, giving great thanks that at least I had the ensuite shower and didn't have to see anyone before that, and got ready for the day. Then, feeling distinctly not quite with it, I made my way down the stairs to the dining room, curious to see who else would be staying at this gracious old place.

I tried a couple of doors at the bottom of the stairs. One was locked, one opened to reveal a TV room. The walls were lined with bookshelves, and a variety of mismatched sofas and easy chairs were strewn around the room. Finally, I opened a door to a large room, filled with long plastic-covered rectangular tables. The room was bright and cheerful with pink floral wallpaper, and small vases of flowers had been set out on the tables. The room was far too cheerful for someone who hadn't had their morning coffee.

Fruit, cereal, and yogurt were set out on a sideboard. Next to that was a place to make toast and then – finally – urns of tea and coffee. The rest of breakfast could wait. I wasn't really interested in that yet. I helped myself to a coffee (instant, but fortunately not the super-cheap stuff) and sat at one end of a table, waiting for the caffeine to kick in.

Slowly, as I warmed up, the room began to warm up too.

First, the little round-faced lady I had met when I checked in, bustled through a swinging door and placed another glass bowl of stewed fruit on the sideboard.

'Hello Luv,' she said. 'Good morning, I should say. How are you this morning?'

I smiled and managed 'Good morning, well thank you. And you?'

'Oh I'm very well. Very well indeed. It's a lovely morning, don't you think? I'm Martha, by the way. I'm sorry, I completely forgot to introduce myself yesterday. Forget my own head next. I must keep setting up.'

I gave the appropriate chuckle and she bustled back through a swinging door and I heard a few clangs and clatters coming from inside. I turned back to my coffee and inner contemplation.

Gradually others made their way into the dining

room and started helping themselves to breakfast. I noticed a bit of a theme as they came in. All of them were all at least 70 years old. There was a wrinkled man in a dog collar who was much older again, somewhere verging on 90, I was sure. I was beginning to feel the odd one out. Quite youthful. The opposite of how I had felt in the group meeting where I'd been the old maid next to the young fresh-faced students. Here, I was a baby.

The conversation in this place was telling, too.

'How's your wife going then?' a woman in a shapeless floral dress asked a man all dressed in beige. Beige trousers, a beige shirt, and a brown cardigan. At least it all matched.

'She's getting there,' he replied. 'They say she'll be up and walking tomorrow or the next day.'

'Well, that's good then,' said a grey-haired gentleman who was spreading marmalade on his toast.

'I hope they don't send us home too soon – it was a six hour drive to get here, she'll need a good bit more energy than she has now for the trip back.' The beige man stopped the vigorous dunking of his tea bag and placed it in the bin.

'Yes, it's quite a journey, isn't it? All the way from Dubbo to Sydney.' This was the floral lady again.

'And how's your husband?' A different woman addressed Mrs Floral. This woman had come in carrying a hefty handbag which she was trying to hang on the back of her chair but it kept slipping off. The back of her chair sloped and wouldn't allow any bag to be hung there, let alone such a large bag stuffed with goodness knows what. Eventually she gave up and placed it on the floor.

Mrs Floral took her toast to her table and sat down with a heartfelt sigh. 'They tell me the operation went well. They said in the end it was a triple bypass. Three blocked arteries! But he came through it well, they tell me. I'm hoping he's able to eat something today. I might go and see what I can buy to tempt him before I head over.'

It took me a while, but I realised that most of the guests in this extremely affordable accommodation were support-people for the residents in the local hospital. It sounded like all of them had driven hours and hours to get here. More hours than you need to get from one end of Tasmania to the other. That was how it was in mainland Australia, I remembered. It is possible to drive anywhere, but you need lots of time to do it. I smiled to myself, remembering hearing of a visiting professor from Europe who thought he could spend a day in Perth and then drive to Sydney and spend the next day there – that he could cover all the capital cities in a week's touring. Not this wide brown land. It takes a long time to get from one end to the other, regardless of whether you travel by train, plane or car.

I got myself a bowl of fruit and muesli and

continued to listen to the health updates. I started to wonder whether I should find somewhere else to stay. Whether I was taking a bed in this place from someone who really needed to stay here to visit their own loved one in hospital.

Suddenly Martha was at my right shoulder. 'Are you here to visit someone at the hospital, Luv?' The question I'd been dreading.

I gave a guilty smile.

'No, actually, I'm here to work at the university. I've come up from Tasmania for a few weeks.'

I felt like an imposter. I had no sick relative, no one dying from cancer to look after. I was here, basically on a pleasure trip, for work. Well, to apply for work, but it was basically the same thing. Maybe I should have left my room for someone who needed it more. I was wondering if Martha would tell me to leave.

But she didn't. She wasn't offended by my answer, and no one else made any judgemental comments either. Instead, she put down the tray of warm muffins on my table and stopped for a chat.

'Well, that's good, Luv. So glad you have work. So many young people don't these days. What area do you work in?' I was aware that everyone in the room was listening to find out who the stranger was. And fair enough too. This place was more than just a hotel. This was a community.

'I'm a scientist,' I said, nice and loudly.

'Oooh that's exciting. A real live scientist. Are you saving the world?' The lady in the floral dress was enthusiastic.

'Always,' I said with a laugh. 'You know us scientists – always out saving the world. Well, at least I'm trying to do my little bit. But it's very little.'

'Oh I'm sure you're doing fine,' Mr Beige joined in. It was like being in a room full of grandparents. They didn't really know what it was all about, but they were thrilled to be there with you, and a part of whatever you were doing. It was comforting.

'One day you might end up like him.' Martha nodded towards the elderly gentleman in the dog collar.

'What do you mean?'

'He's heading off to Government House this morning to receive an award from the Governor himself.'

'No way. That's awesome. Congratulations.' I smiled in his direction.

The old man looked modestly down his nose. He didn't look like he was up for a lot of conversation this morning. But I was too curious to let this go. And I was sure Martha would be happy to tell me all the gossip.

'What is the award for?'

'He's done heaps of work with immigrants – helping them settle in. It's what he spent his whole life doing, looking after others. It's so good that he's finally getting recognition.'

The old man didn't seem too sure he agreed with that. He looked like quietly doing his work was all that he wanted to be allowed to do. Saints are often like that, I thought, and they are not often allowed to be. It annoys the rest of us who need all the encouragement we can get.

Martha picked up the tray of muffins again and offered them to everyone around the room. She asked everyone about their situation, seeming to know each one and to care about their problems like they were family.

I thoughtfully finished my muffin and piled my dishes in the plastic tray left out for the purpose near the kitchen door. I was inspired by the saintliness of the old man, by the care Martha showed to everyone and by the self-sacrifice of these people who were serving their sick spouses. I didn't have a sick spouse (or any spouse), but decided to spend the day reaching out to those around me as I did my work. Feeling virtuous, as if I had been to church and got all fired up, I tripped lightly up the stairs to grab my bags and get started on the day.

9

From my position outside the locked glass doors of the lab looking in, the whole place looked deserted. I knocked on the door anyway, hoping that someone was around, maybe working at a fume hood where I couldn't see them. I really needed to get set up with a swipe-card as soon as possible, and wifi access would be a good idea as well. But that all required paperwork, filling out of forms and delivering them to the right people. And that took time. I wanted to get going on the lab work too, and that was more important. But access to the lab was essential.

What to do first? I decided I would make a time with Robbie to find my old samples and then do the admin tasks around that. If I could ever get into the office.

Tony's head popped around the corner of a fume hood and, once he recognised me, he gave me a smile and walked over to open the door. We shared our 'good mornings' and he took himself back to his experiment and back to work. I walked through the lab, past the yellow cabinets and into the office wondering what state my desk would be in.

By some miracle, my desk was clear, the papers now stacked in precariously high piles forming a fortress around Rebekah. I wondered how long it had taken her to get things to that state. She was working in a tiny space in the middle of her desk, writing comments in red pen on what looked like a first-year student's lab book. (I could tell by the way the page was laid out – typed questions with boxes for the answers. And by the answers themselves, which were written in large childish handwriting with the fewest possible words for each answer.)

'Good morning. Thanks so much for making space for me,' I said.

Rebekah looked at me cautiously.

'Are you being sarcastic?'

'Not at all.' I rushed to reassure her. 'It looks like you don't have enough room for all that you do.'

'You could say that,' she responded gloomily.

'I'm only here for two weeks. You'll get this space back soon enough.'

'Or someone else will come and take it. No, don't worry, it's not your fault. I just need to figure out how to organise myself.'

'Well, I'll leave you to it. You look quite busy enough.'

'Thanks.'

Robbie wasn't there. I sat and waited, watching the office gradually fill with people. Some of the students were all business. They picked up their record books, pulled on their lab coats and headed straight into the lab to do experiments. Others sat at their desks, checking email and social media, and chatting with each other.

Eventually Robbie blew in, dumping his bag on the desk.

'Stupid bloody train drivers,' he complained.

'What's up?' I asked.

'Do you know they get paid a ridiculous wage, a hundred thousand, and all they do is stand in that little cubicle up the front. And then they can't even keep the trains running on time. I mean, how hard can it be?'

He threw his jacket on the back of the chair, pulled notebooks out of his bag and slammed them on the desk.

'Gray's going to tell me off for being late again. I can't help it if the trains are so stupidly late.' Cursing and grumbling to himself he found a pen and the notepad he wanted and turned to leave again.

'Um …' I said.

'What?' he snapped and then immediately changed his tone. 'Sorry Alicia, I'm just a bit frustrated this morning.'

'When do you think would be a good time to find those samples?'

'Oh … right … well I'm off to a meeting right now, but maybe after morning tea?'

'Sounds great. Thanks Robbie.'

'Sure, no problem,' he muttered and then raced back out through the lab, almost running, but not quite. No running was allowed in the lab and Robbie, the lab manager, knew that rule well.

OK, so that meant I wasn't doing lab work first thing. It was time to take myself down to reception and get the paperwork sorted out.

10

Seeing as I was leaving the lab, I thought a coffee might be in order too. I know, any excuse for a coffee, but my virtuous plans for getting work done had been thwarted, so I figured I was now free to enjoy a bit more time off. I searched through my bag for my purse and the sight of the key to my room at St Catherine's reminded me of my resolution to reach out to my office mates. I looked at Rebekah, buried head-high in paperwork and I remembered the nasty looks Wei and Mike had given each other through her group meeting presentation. The eye-rolls and raised eyebrows must make her feel uncomfortable, if not miserable, day to day. Maybe she was the person I should be reaching out to. I could try to make her day a little brighter. I decided to give it a go.

'Would you like to come and join me for a coffee?' I asked.

'Oh ...' She looked shocked. 'Um ... I have a lot to do.' She waved her hand vaguely at her desk.

'It won't be a long one. I have a lot to do too. But I reckon we could make time for a short coffee.'

She dithered.

'My shout,' I said. 'The caffeine will make the work easier afterwards.'

She gave in.

'OK,' she said, and put down her pen.

It was a few more minutes before we left the office. Rebekah had to find her keys and swipe-card, and her phone was hidden under a pile of paper that had slid sideways on her desk to cover it. It was a good thing that her phone case was such a bright pink – if it had been less gaudy we might have never found it. Eventually we made it out.

Rebekah seemed almost furtive as we left the office. She kept looking around like she was in trouble. Like she was sneaking out of class in high school.

'Are you OK?' I asked.

'I'm just … are you sure it's OK to go for coffee so early?'

'Who is going to tell you off? You'll make up the time, I'm sure. And it's good for us neighbours to get to know each other.'

We were both adults. What was she worried about?

She laughed self-consciously.

'I guess so. I just feel like I should be working all the time. I get worried that … that someone will notice and get on my case.'

'I wouldn't worry about it. I'm sure that everyone here goes for coffee at some stage.'

'Yes, but I think I have more to do than everyone else. At least, I can't seem to get it all done.'

'Maybe while I'm here we could work on some strategies for you. I'm happy to help you get organised.'

Wow, I *was* feeling virtuous. But, to be honest, I could see that a few organisational methods put into place consistently could really help Rebekah. I didn't think it would take much of my time to help her a whole lot.

'I just hope Mike doesn't see us,' she said, looking over her shoulder again. It was weird, this high school mentality. I reacted like I was a teenager myself.

'Who is he to tell us what to do? We're adults.'

'Well, he's the group boss really. I mean, Prof Gray is, but Mike does all the telling off. Unless we've done something really bad. Then we have to go to Prof Gray's office, like it's the headmaster's room.'

We bypassed the long line of students waiting for takeaway coffee. Instead we took a seat in the café section at the back, and ordered our coffee there. I was determined to make this a proper break for Rebekah, she looked like she needed it.

Over our coffee I tried to find a subject that we had in common. We ended up chatting about mistakes made in the lab. About people stealing NMR tubes from others, or taking up more than their share of fume hood space. About washing up not being done, and samples being stored incorrectly.

Looking back over my time at various universities, I had a wealth of great stories to tell.

'I remember when the wrong nitrogen cylinder was being used for the glove box where the air-sensitive samples were being kept. They used a nitrogen cylinder that was only 90% pure and someone's samples were destroyed. About two years of their work down the drain,' I said.

Rebekah gasped. 'What happened?'

'They got a new cylinder. And the student repeated all her work.'

'Did the person get kicked out?'

I laughed at that.

'Kicked out? No, of course not. It was an honest mistake.'

She looked down and swirled her cup of coffee.

'I always feel like I'm on the edge of being kicked out of here,' she said.

I didn't know what to say to that. In my experience it took a lot of wrong-doing to get kicked out of a PhD. A lot. But she seemed to be honestly scared.

'Did you always want to come here to the University of Sydney?' I asked.

Maybe it was just the institution that was so precious to her. Sydney was, after all, one of the top universities in the country.

'Yes ... well ... sort of.' Rebekah stared out of the window for a moment, her eyes went distant, and I wondered what she was imagining. 'At least, my parents really wanted me to come. My Mum, she really wanted me to come. Really wanted me to make something out of my life, to leave home. She was so insistent, and I was so glad to get that scholarship. I don't know what I would have done if I didn't get it. Dad, he …' She broke off, and glanced at me. 'I mean, it was good to get it, yeah? But now I feel like I need to work so hard to prove myself. I get a bit tired sometimes.'

There was obviously a story behind that, but I didn't think now was the time to probe. I thought I'd concentrate on the problem at hand.

'I don't think you really need to work absolutely all the time. I mean, not weekends and evenings. You need regular breaks or you burn out. I tried doing most of my PhD from nine to five rather than working all the week long and I got it done in good time. I think really that the same thing should be possible for everyone.'

She shook her head.

'I'd never get everything done just working nine to five. It would be impossible. I come in every weekend and do a bit more lab work.'

I was horrified. Every weekend? She worked every weekend?

'How long has it been since you've had a day off?' I asked.

'Oh about three months I think.'

'Three months without a weekend?' She nodded. I shook my head. 'Well, I really hope … no, I'm sure it will pay off for you.'

I wasn't at all sure. But I didn't feel like I could convince her to do things differently. Maybe over the course of the next few weeks I could help her to make a change. Maybe helping Rebekah to manage her time would be the big and wonderful thing I could do during my time here. (As well as, of course, getting myself a job. I needed to remember that priority too.) But there was no way that everyone else in the research group was working quite as hard as Rebekah was. And, truthfully, she shouldn't have to work that hard.

I probed a bit more.

'Is it the research that is taking all the time? Or is it the teaching? Are you doing demonstrating for the undergraduate students as well?'

'I … I'm not allowed to do demonstrating.' Rebekah looked down at the table and fiddled with her teaspoon.

'Really?' That was a new one. She was really opening up my eyes. 'Just you? Or is everyone in the group forbidden to teach?'

'No, no. Just me. Well, me and Tony. It's a clause in our scholarship. We're just supposed to research.'

'That makes sense. I'm glad you've got that taken off your plate. It sounds like you have quite enough to do.'

She bit her lip.

'Yeah, I do really. And it's a bit of a risk for me to come in on the weekends.'

'A risk? How?' Did she leave her house unattended too much? Was the cost of travel using up all her scholarship money?

'I have this allergy.'

'An allergy?' I frowned. Why would an allergy make weekend work risky?

'Yes, I'm highly allergic to latex.'

'Latex? I've never heard of an allergy to that before.'

'Well, it's true.' Rebekah pouted defensively. 'Remember? Robbie said so in the group meeting. I'm not just trying to get out of washing up in the lab, like some people think.'

'Of course not. I believe you. Sorry.' I was chastened.

'I don't really like coming in on the weekends just in case … in case something happens. There's usually someone else about, but sometimes I'm alone in the lab, and what if something went wrong? Who would be here to help me? But then I have to get the work done so I usually come in anyway.'

'Is your allergy severe?'

I had gone from disbelieving to curious. We all use latex in the lab; I expected to be donning latex gloves that very afternoon as I played with my samples. But if you had a severe allergy …

'Oh yes. I've ended up in hospital a few times. If I touch latex I just swell up and break out in hives. It can stop me breathing.'

'Wow! That's bad! Do you carry an epipen with you?' I looked at the pile of stuff that she had taken from her desk that was now sitting on the table.

Keys, phone, swipe-card, but nothing that looked like an epipen. Maybe she needed a nice handbag.

'I keep one in my desk drawer. Everyone in the group knows it's there.'

'A latex allergy,' I mused aloud. 'That's fascinating.'

'I guess it's fascinating if it's not happening to you. I don't like it. I wish I could stop working weekends. I could too, if only …'

She took a sip of her coffee, eyes staring at the milky liquid like it held great wisdom.

'Can I tell you something?' she asked eventually.

'Sure.'

'It's … um … you can't tell anyone else.'

'Who would I tell? I don't know anyone here. Well, except Robbie.' Her face blanched and I back-pedalled. 'I won't tell him though. No, I can keep a secret. You can tell me.'

'There's a reason why I'm working so hard,' she began, then stopped as a shadow loomed over the table.

'Good morning, girls.' It was Mike. Mike who was nothing but rude and uncommunicative had chosen that moment to come and chat with us.

'Good morning,' I said.

'Taking a little time off, are we?'

'Just a morning coffee to get us into the zone.' I carried the conversation. Rebekah was studying her coffee now like it was the key to the universe. I could have killed Mike.

'Well, don't stay too long. Busy, busy,' he said,

then wandered over to the crowd waiting for their takeaway cups.

I frowned at his retreating back. Way to undo all my hard work. I looked back at Rebekah and tried to pick up where we had left off.

'What's the reason why you're working hard?' I asked.

'Oh, don't worry about it,' she said. And then with more conviction, 'No, I'm sure it's just because I'm disorganised.'

She took a final gulp of her coffee.

'Thanks for the break. I had better get back to work now.' She stood. I looked at my half-finished coffee. Did I have to leave now too? No, I was going to show her a good example by staying and finishing my coffee. I stayed seated and looked up at her.

'If you ever want to talk with me about organisational strategies or family or ... or anything else, I'm here for you,' I said with as friendly a smile as I could muster.

I watched Mike watch Rebekah as she walked out the door. What a task master! He couldn't even let her have a coffee with a friend. But he could have one for himself, obviously. He was rapidly becoming the person I liked least in the group.

I didn't invite him over to my table. But I thought a lot about his attitude as I finished my coffee. It went quickly too, drinking by yourself isn't as much fun as chatting with a friend. And before I knew it,

I was back at reception, collecting all the forms I needed to get my own swipe-card for the lab door.

11

The rest of the day was a little uncomfortable. Rebekah was working at the desk next to mine but when I tried to chat with her, or say anything at all, she brushed me off or avoided my eyes. I was really wondering what I had done to make her so upset with me. I had only tried to help, and I only used up twenty minutes of her time, if that. But apparently I was *persona non grata*. So much for making someone's life better.

It would have helped if I'd had another neighbour, but I had Rebekah's desk on one side, and the wall of yellow cupboards on the other. So it was chat to Rebekah, or nothing. I could hear friendly conversation all around, but whether it was because I had asked for that extra group meeting, or just because I was sitting next to Rebekah and we weren't talking, whatever the reason, I was not included in the little chats. I felt almost invisible.

I put my head down and finished my paperwork, and when Robbie came back he showed me the cupboards in the lab where my samples were likely to be stored. I spent the afternoon pulling out boxes and looking through vials trying to find the glass tubes labelled with my handwriting. It was dirty, fiddly work. I stood every few minutes to go to the sink and rinse my hands. I would have been happier with gloves on to guard against the dust and goodness-knows-what contamination on other people's samples, but Robbies 'no gloves' policy held and I nearly washed the skin off my hands trying to keep myself clean and safe.

By five o'clock I figured I'd had enough of this horrible day. I wasn't going to stay late. I packed my notebooks and folders into my bag along with my laptop, and prepared to leave. Rebekah talked to me then, for the first time since the morning.

'Are you leaving?' she asked.

'Yeah, I'm done.'

'Would you mind if I used your desk this evening to put some papers on? I promise I'll clear them all by tomorrow.'

'Sure. No problem. I'm taking all this home with me. You can have the whole desk overnight.' I swung my bag onto my shoulder, and wondered if I should say more. Would it be helpful to lecture her about working late again? Would it be helpful to let her know that 5 p.m. was actually the end of the work day?

I decided to leave the argument for the day. I'd given her a talk over coffee in the morning and I could do the same tomorrow. Besides, most of the other students were still working away at their desks. But it was time for me to go. I needed to get away from the uncomfortable atmosphere. I took the fire escape stairs and breathed deeply of the cool evening air. Freedom. Space. I was going to make the most of it, before 9 a.m. tomorrow when I would find out if Rebekah had actually cleared my desk again or not.

After a lonely meal in a Thai restaurant on King Street, I was needing a little bit of comfort. Well actually, a big bit of comfort by the time I got back to St Catherine's. I wanted a nice hot drink and a cosy corner to drink it in.

I went downstairs to see what I could find.

The dining room with its ten long tables, plastic cloths, and hard wooden chairs felt huge and impersonal. But I found myself a cup and dug around in the cupboard under the urn to find a tin of hot chocolate. I dished two teaspoons into a mug and then, feeling naughty, added a heaped teaspoon of sugar. The hot water was there ready for me to use, but there was no milk. It was time to make a foray into the kitchen and find a fridge.

The stainless-steel kitchen was a relief after the bright pink and floral of the dining room walls. A high stainless steel bench, a stainless steel industrial dishwasher, a large stainless steel oven and a black gas cooktop. Everything was functional, nothing was decorative. And it was easy to find where the milk would be stored.

I opened the fridge door and a voice behind me said, 'Hello dear, everything OK?'

I nearly dropped my hot chocolate.

'Hi Martha,' I said sheepishly. 'Is this OK? I just wanted a hot drink.'

'Oh sure, Luv, that's fine. A hot chocolate is so nice at night, isn't it? So comforting. Are you feeling alright?'

I melted before her motherly face. It had been so long since I had been mothered by anyone.

'I've just had a bit of a hard day.'

'Well, hang on a tick, Luv, I'll get myself a cuppa too, and you can tell me all about it.'

We didn't go back into the dining room. We sat on high stools at a corner of the bench in the kitchen (it was pretty amazing to watch Martha lever herself up there) and sipped our hot drinks, and I poured out all my annoyance with Mike, my concern for Rebekah, and my frustration with myself.

'I was going to be all wonderful and self-sacrificing, and then … well I must have done something wrong. I don't think I can ask her to come for coffee again.'

'Oh, you did a good job, dear.'

I looked at her questioningly.

'Well, that's what I think. She had a coffee break, didn't she? You can only be responsible for what you do, not for what others do.' Martha patted my knee comfortingly.

'Well, that's true. But if I was a good friend I'd be forcing her to have a break. She works far too hard.'

I fiddled with my mug, staring at the bench top.

'Oh Luv, you know she has to decide for herself. It reminds me of a lovely lady we had here for a while. Her sister was in hospital, and she wouldn't eat. And the lady here, she was nearly starving herself in sympathy, worrying herself half to death. I had to take her aside and give her a good talking to. And when she started taking care of herself and letting her sister make her own decisions, it meant that she had the energy to look at the situation properly. And then she could talk to the sister's doctor and all, and in the end they figured out food allergies and all sorts of wonderful stuff. It all came right. But just worrying about it doesn't fix anything.'

'I guess so.'

'What is your girl working so hard at? Is she saving the world too?' Martha smiled at me but I didn't give an answering smile, because that question had been bothering me all afternoon.

'To tell the truth, I don't know. Like, if I didn't hear her say she was in at uni working every weekend, I would have thought she was stuffing around doing very little. She seems so behind with all her work, and in such a panic. I don't know how she works that hard, and doesn't get ahead.'

'Hmmm, that's tricky, isn't it? Maybe instead of coffee dates, she needs lessons.'

'Time management lessons? Possibly. They don't teach those in a PhD but maybe they should.'

'We don't learn things all by ourselves, do we?'

I shook my head. It looked like this wrinkled and wonderful lady had learned a whole lot that I hadn't learned. Maybe I needed to take lessons from her.

We finished our hot drinks and Martha levered herself off the tall stool and patted me on the leg. 'Now, you don't have to worry, dear. I'm sure all of that will just sort itself out. You just take care of yourself, be a friend as you can to all of them, and let them deal with their own problems.'

I nodded. 'Thanks Martha, I will.'

'And you keep me posted as to how it all goes.'

I smiled. I guessed that this would give her stories to tell others later. And if it did, well, no harm done.

12

As I walked to work the next morning I saw a commotion up ahead. Flashing lights greeted me – red and blue, police and ambulance. This looked like a real emergency. Someone had kicked the ants nest of the chemistry building causing people to spill out and wander aimlessly around the avenue. I quickened my pace, hoping I could find out something, and hoping against hope that I didn't know the person involved.

I jostled my way to the front of a small crowd at the main door to hear the policeman stationed there say that we were all to keep out. That he was sure it wouldn't be much longer, but they would take as long as they needed to. That he was sorry but he would not be giving out any information at this stage, a press conference would be held shortly if it was necessary and staff would be briefed accordingly.

I wondered how I was going to find out what was going on? I wasn't going to be told anything by the police. And I wasn't sure that I'd get briefed by the university. I wasn't officially staff – just a visitor, and no-one would officially tell me anything. The curiosity was like a mosquito bite, an itch just needing to be scratched.

But there wasn't much that I could do straight away, so I decided to go for a coffee while I waited for the building to reopen. In my opinion, time spent obtaining and drinking a coffee was never time wasted. And also, thanks to the floor to ceiling windows in the café, I could keep an eye on things at the same time.

As I waited for my order to be filled I looked around to see if I could see someone from the group, someone I knew. A few emergency personnel were attending to someone on a park bench, and as they moved away I saw that the someone was Robbie. Why was he the centre of attention? Had he been hurt? Was he the cause of all the commotion? I bounced with impatience. Robbie was someone I could easily talk to and he might have the information I wanted. He was involved somehow. Why weren't they quicker making these drinks?

Finally, I heard my name called and I picked up my cup and raced across the avenue to where Robbie was sitting.

'Robbie, are you ok? Do you need coffee?' I asked. I figured I could go and order one for him if it would help.

'Coffee, that's exactly what I need.' Robbie swiped the cup out of my hand and took a large swig before I could say anything. He looked so grateful that I felt OK with my sacrifice. I'd go back and order another one shortly. Right now my curiosity was more important than even my caffeine fix.

'What's going on? Has there been an accident?'

'You might say that.' Robbie took another swig of the hot coffee, like it was medicine. 'I guess you'll hear soon enough. Everyone will know soon. Rebekah has died.'

'Rebekah? What?' I couldn't believe my ears. 'Are you sure? How did you find out?'

'I found her.'

'You found her?' I sat on the bench next to him. My legs felt weak.

'In the lab. When I came in this morning there she was, lying on the floor in between two rows of fume hoods.'

'That must have been an incredible shock.'

'The ambulance people have been treating me for shock, but they don't make good coffee.' Robbie tried a wan smile, but it didn't really sit right on his face. Yes, coffee, I really needed one now. I nearly took my cup back out of Robbie's hands to have a sip myself.

'What happened? Do they know? Was it an accident?' I really had to know. Only yesterday I'd been trying to make her life better, and now …

'I really don't know, she was … she was slumped on the floor, against the wall, next to her fume hood. All crumpled up and she looked, she looked awful … like, swollen. And all puffy and red and blotchy. I don't know how it happened.'

'I think I might.' I blurted. The thought had just popped into my head.

'Really? How would you know, you didn't even see her.'

I knew that, but still.

'I just wonder if it had anything to do with her latex allergy.'

Robbie nodded slowly.

'That's right, she is allergic, isn't she? Or …' he hesitated and looked at the ground. 'She was.'

'Was there any latex around her? Do you remember seeing any?'

Robbie shook his head.

'I've been trying not to think about her at all, trying to put it out of my mind, you know? But it keeps coming back, her face. I just looked at her face and …' he broke off.

'Yeah, I can imagine. Horrendous.'

'You have no idea.' He took another sip of the coffee. I was pleased to see that he'd slowed down a little. He was drinking it like a drink now, not like a lifeline.

'I guess someone in charge needs to know about her allergy,' I said. 'Would you like me to tell them?'

Robbie thought for a bit.

'Maybe. You could try I guess. It's written in her records somewhere but it wouldn't hurt to let them know.'

'I'll give it a go.'

I patted Robbie awkwardly on the shoulder. He looked like a wreck and I wanted to give him a hug and let him cry but I was pretty sure he wouldn't really appreciate that.

Instead, I stood, pulled myself together and found the nearest uniformed officer.

'Um, excuse me?'

'No one is allowed in at this time Ma'am. You'll have to wait until the building is reopened.' The officer spoke like he was playing a prerecorded message.

'Yeah, I get that, it's just that – '

'I'm sorry Ma'am, that's my orders,' interrupted the officer. 'You can wait just like everyone else.'

'I just have some information …' I tried again.

'It doesn't matter how important your work is, you'll have to wait.'

There was no talking to him, I realised. And he probably wasn't the right person to tell anyway. I gave up and wandered back to see how Robbie was.

There were more people with him now. Members of the research group had started to turn up for work and were hanging around in a group with Robbie at the centre. He was starting to become a bit less fragile; I could see him building the walls around himself that he needed to stay upright. He looked over at me.

'How did it go?'

I shook my head. 'He called me Ma'am – I hate being called Ma'am, makes me feel old. I'm not a Ma'am, am I?'

'Ha. So he didn't listen, then…'

'Nope, told me that he had his orders and that

I was not to enter the building. Wouldn't listen to a word I said. So I'll try again later if I can find the right person to tell. I wonder if there will be a briefing of staff or something.'

'There will be something, I'll let you know, see if I can sneak you in.'

'I'd just like to be helpful if that's possible.'

'We'll work out something.'

'Are you going to go home?' Tony asked Robbie, though his tone of voice suggested he wanted him to stay.

'You had a big shock. You should go home. Get well.' That was Yumi, a little more compassionate.

But Robbie shook his head and stood up, dropping the coffee cup in the bin at the side of the bench.

'You know, I'd prefer to get on with some work, I think. If I'm just sitting around thinking, I'll keep remembering … No, I'll head back up there as soon as they open the doors. Back on the horse, you know?'

There were nods of agreement. Though I heard Wei grumble, 'I would have taken the week. Why not when you have a ready-made excuse like this?'

I told them all I was getting myself a coffee and as I turned to cross the avenue, the ambulance started its engine and the surrounding crowd parted to let it through and then moved, as one, towards the doors of the building. It was time to get on with the day. But I needed a coffee first, and I was going to have a lot to tell Martha when I got home that night.

13

Paper cup in hand (I really must buy a Keep Cup, I told myself) I walked up the two flights of stairs to the lab, but when I got there the whole group was standing around outside the door. All the students were there, but Robbie and Mike were missing, and Prof Gray wasn't there either.

I sidled up to Sofia who was standing at the back of the disorganised group.

'What's going on?' I asked.

'We can't get in, see?' She pointed towards the lab and I looked over the shoulders of the students in front of me to see that the blue and white tape signifying a crime scene was taped across the door. And just in case we didn't know exactly what that meant, a big 'no entry' sign was hanging from the tape as well. The lab was off-limits.

'So what are we going to do?'

'We don't know,' she shrugged.

'How long do we have to stay out for?'

'Don't know.' She shrugged again.

'Do we know anything?' I asked.

Tony laughed. 'Not so as you'd notice.'

'Robbie, Mike, and Prof Gray are talking with police now,' Sofia said, more helpfully. 'They told us to stay here until they come back. So we are just waiting.'

Great. I hate waiting.

All of the group were there. It had been well after nine by the time we were allowed into the building and everyone had expected to start the day by now. Some of the students – Wei, Sofia, Yusuf – were now hoping for the day off. They were chatting in fits and starts, playing on their phones, wasting time. Tony and Sahar stood near the door, compulsively checking their watches, crossing and uncrossing their arms, even tapping their feet in their impatience to get into the lab and start their work. They looked down the corridor so many times to see if the leaders were coming back that they looked like the guard prairie dogs on a David Attenborough documentary.

I felt like someone was missing (not just Rebekah, someone else too), though I was having trouble remembering all the group members. I thought about all the group meeting talks from the day before, picturing each student, and eventually worked out that Yumi wasn't here with the rest of the group. I was just about to nudge Sofia and ask her where she was (expecting another shrug and 'I don't know') when the door to the bathroom opened and Yumi came out. She was sniffing and carefully touching tears away from her eyes, trying not to smudge her makeup.

I rushed over to give her comfort, a little disturbed that not one other person from the group did the same.

'Yumi, are you OK?'

It may have been the wrong thing to say. Her face crumpled and the tears fell in earnest.

'Oh, I … I can't believe it,' she said with a sob.

'You were Rebekah's friend?'

'She was so nice to me.'

I sat her on the stairs and put my arm around her as she let the tears fall.

The rest of the group finally noticed her distress and crowded around us to offer various platitudes and words of sympathy. Some appropriate, some not so much.

'You will have the whole fume hood to yourself now,' from Wei. Really not helpful. Who cares about bench space when you have lost a friend?

'We won't get bothered by her horrible ring tone anymore either. I won't miss her phone going off all the time.' Another look-on-the-bright-side oh-so-unhelpful comment from Tony.

Others made more conventional, 'there there, you'll be alright,' comments. In the end I suggested they all leave us alone, saying that she probably just needed a good cry.

And eventually, as they saw Robbie and Mike coming down the corridor, they did leave us alone.

Mike spoke first. 'Right. The police say they need us to stay out of the lab and office for the whole day. They have promised to be finished with it by tomorrow but for today we can't go in.'

That led to a range of responses. There was a fist pump and a 'Yes!' from Yusuf, but Tony and Sahar were much more put out.

'Can we use the conference room to work in instead?' asked Tony.

'You can, but you can't take anything at all out of the lab or the office.'

'We can't move our computers then.'

'Nope, nothing at all.' This was Robbie. 'I tried, really I did. But they are sticking firm. Just take the day off. Go home and recover.'

That was good advice, and while a few of the students made plans to watch a movie together, I rubbed Yumi's back and told her to go home and drink something warm. And not to come back until she was ready.

'You need to allow yourself to take some time to grieve. Do you have someone at home to talk to?'

'I can ring my parents in Japan.'

'That's a good idea. You do that. And then watch some silly TV, and just look after yourself. You'll be OK.'

Yumi gave a big sniff and nodded.

'And maybe you should wash your face before you head off,' I suggested. This got a watery smile.

'That is what I did before you ask me if I am OK. So maybe you go, and then I wash so you don't ask me, and I don't cry again.'

I smiled at that.

'Good idea.'

I gave her one last hug and followed the rest of the group down the stairs.

I was seriously grateful that, unlike Tony and Sahar, I could set myself up at St Catherine's and get work done. I had my laptop and all my work with me in my bag. I couldn't do anything with the samples in the lab, but I could work on the seminar presentation I needed to make on interview day, and I could think about the interview itself. It wouldn't be a wasted day even though I couldn't do the lab-based work. I slung my bag back on my shoulder, and headed back to my temporary home.

14

There was no desk in my little room so I set up my laptop on one of the tables in the dining room. I found a table where I could stare out the window to the garden beyond, and I made myself comfortable.

I thought I'd get some good work done. I didn't think I'd need to take time to grieve like Yumi. But in reality I reckon I was doing equal amounts of staring out the window and working on my presentation. There was a bit to process. I mean, I didn't know Rebekah well by any stretch, but to have coffee with someone one day, and have her turn up dead on the next, that was a lot to come to terms with. Thinking wasn't coming very easily to me. But I counted my blessings. At least when I remembered her face it was the face of a healthy and happy person (well, happy-ish in the case of Rebekah) rather than the horrible sight that Robbie described. I wondered how he was coping with everything. Probably with the help of a whisky or two, something that St Catherine's didn't have on the premises.

However, St Catherine's did have tea, and I got up to make myself a strong cup.

I heard the squeak of old door hinges and Martha came in to the dining room, giving me her welcoming smile when she saw me.

'Hello Luv, what are you doing here today? I thought you were long gone to work.'

'There will be no work happening today,' I said.

'What? Did something happen? An explosion in the laboratory? A flood? A strike?'

'Sort of. I turned up at the university and found out that one of the students died last night.'

'And you're so sad you can't work?' Martha looked confused. 'But you only met them this week.'

'No, it's not that.' I smiled. 'She died in the lab in an accident. The police have cordoned it off. None of us is allowed in there today.'

Martha gestured for me to follow her as she went into the kitchen and turned the kettle on. It looked like her response to tragedy was the same as mine. Time for a nice strong cup of tea.

'How did she die? What happened? Did she poison herself? Was there an explosion?' Martha was full of questions, and not giving me any time for the answers.

'Martha. What is it with you and explosions today? No, she died ... actually I don't know for sure. I only know what I've been told, that her face was all puffy and stuff. But I think she died of an allergic reaction.'

'Ooooh that's not good.' Martha pulled two large mugs out of the cupboard and sat them on the bench next to the kettle.

'No, it's not. But she thought something like that would happen.'

She leaned back against the bench and looked at me.

'She thought it would happen? How do you know she thought that? Are you reading minds now?'

I shook my head. 'It was Rebekah who died. The girl I had coffee with yesterday.'

'The same girl?'

I nodded. 'The very same.'

'Well, that's a bit of a shock. And she told you she thought she might die?'

'No, not as much, she told me that she was allergic to latex and she was worried that she'd have an allergic reaction in the lab sometime when no one was around to help her.'

'And then it happened, that very same night. What are the chances?'

The kettle neared boiling and Martha pulled out two tea bags and put them in the cups.

'I know. It's awful.' I leaned up against the bench and let Martha do all the work.

She filled the mugs with water and dunked the tea bags thoughtfully for a few minutes. Then, as she put the bags into the bin she said, 'At least you have me for an alibi.'

'What?' I was confused.

Martha pulled milk out of the fridge and poured 'just a drop' into each cup.

'When the police investigate, you can say you were here having a hot chocolate with me. Your alibi is firm.'

I shook my head, trying to understand.

'What on earth are you talking about?'

She sat my hot tea on the bench next to me.

'Don't you think it sounds just a little bit suspicious? One minute, here she is, telling you all about her allergy, the next she's dead, from the allergy she was just telling you about. It's a good thing you were here having a hot chocolate with me. That's all.'

Now I knew how Nate had felt when I had jumped to a similar conclusion before. If there's a tragic death, that's quite enough to cope with, without someone saying that it's a murder. Deciding that the death was suspicious was just unnecessary.

'Martha, you've watched too much Miss Marple.' I hoped she wouldn't take offence, and she didn't.

Instead, she laughed, a good belly laugh.

'You're probably right,' she said. 'But Alicia, if the lab is such a dangerous place for her to work, why have all the health and safety people let her work there?'

'It's not really a dangerous place to work,' I started with my patronising little speech that I'd given so many times before when people asked about the 'dangerous' chemistry lab.

'We all know how to use the chemicals and equipment, we all do risk assessments before we start anything.'

And then just to be sure, I added, 'And as far as Rebekah's allergy goes, well, Robbie (that's the lab manager) doesn't like us to use gloves at all, and the latex gloves are kept in the cupboard, and only brought out if they are really needed.'

'Aha!' Martha was triumphant. 'Tell me then, how did she have the allergic reaction if the gloves were nowhere to be found. How did she come across them? You can't have it both ways.'

I sighed. 'Look, can we just say this was a tragic death and leave it at that?'

Martha nodded. 'If you need to, dear.'

'I just think it was so sad. She was talking with me about how desperately she wanted to come to Sydney Uni, or how desperate her father was for her to come, anyway. How hard she was working. How difficult it was for her. But she was giving it a good go, and now she's gone. It's really sad.'

'Yes, a life cut short. It is always very sad to lose someone so young. To lose all that potential.'

We sat in comfortable silence for a while, sipping our hot mugs of tea. It was very sad to have lost Rebekah, but I was grateful to have a friend like Martha to comfort me through it.

15

'So are you proud of me, Nate?' I asked as I scraped the dinner plate clean with my fork.

'Proud of you for what?'

'Not jumping to conclusions. Here is Martha talking alibis and suspicious deaths and I just sat calmly and told her not to worry. See, I'm learning.'

Nate laughed. 'Yes, Alicia, I'm very proud of you. It didn't do you much good though, did it?'

'As it turned out, no. But I tried to stay away. I really did.'

'You didn't think it was a murder straight away?' Jan asked doubtfully.

I bristled a bit. I didn't think that every single death was a murder. Truly. I just had come across a few murders recently. But that wasn't my fault. Though maybe this one was.

'At that point I didn't know what to think. I hadn't seen anything, I didn't really know the people I worked with, not even Rebekah though I'd tried to get to know her. I guess I might have been worried they'd hold a stranger accountable but I didn't think this had anything to do with me. Not then. I was trying not to think about it at all.'

Jan cleared the plates and wine glasses away and came back from the kitchen with a plate of cake that she put on the coffee table in the lounge room.

'Nate can make some coffees. You and I should move to the comfy chairs now,' she said.

'I'll try not to fall asleep. Comfy chairs, full stomach. This is wonderful.'

'That's what the coffee is for – to keep you awake until you finish this story.'

'I'll do my best,' I said. It was so good to get it all out. To tell my good friends the whole story. I cut myself a large slice of cake and put my thoughts into order to keep going.

16

After that nice chat with Martha I went back to my laptop to get working again. I checked my phone and found an email from Prof Gray, written to the whole group. It said that there would be a group meeting at 9 a.m. sharp the next morning to discuss the situation before we would be allowed back into the lab. His email ended with an uncharacteristically firm statement, 'Lateness will not be tolerated.'

So that night I set myself an extra alarm, just to be sure I woke on time the next day. I slept dreadfully, as one does when an on-time wake-up is essential the next day. But I was definitely at work on time.

I slipped into the conference room right on nine and sat myself next to Robbie in the back row of the hard plastic seats.

'Did you have a good day off yesterday?' I whispered.

'Didn't get a day off at all,' he murmured in return. 'Spent the whole day talking with police.'

'With police? Why?'

But then we were called to order and the meeting started.

I expected Prof Gray to start the conversation, but he remained seated and a tall angular woman stood at the front of the room instead.

I nudged Robbie again, 'Who's she?' I whispered.

'Sandison. Head of School,' he replied shortly.

'Thank you all for coming,' the woman said. 'I'm sure you are all devastated at the loss of one of your group.' I looked around for signs of devastation. Yumi was nodding and wiping her eyes, but I could also see Mike shrugging and Wei rolling his eyes. The rest of the group were stoney-faced.

'The university is taking this situation very seriously and we will be working with the Work Health and Safety team to put measures in place to protect any other vulnerable members of our research teams and students. For now, Geoffrey will be telling you about immediate changes in your laboratory.'

It took me a minute to remember that Prof Gray's first name was Geoffrey, not 'Prof'. But of course it was. And maybe sometime I would graduate to calling him something different from what all the students called him. But then, maybe not. For me Prof Gray was his name.

I reset my focus back on the Head of School.

'I would also like to let you know that grief counselling is available. The email address for making an appointment will be sent to you this morning.

'I will convey to the whole department a clear message about the critical priority of safety for our university. This incident reminds us that our department does many interesting and risky things, and our standard must be that we will not have people injured doing those things. An investigation will be held into this incident, and our efforts to improve safety in the department will be redoubled.

'Thank you for your safety efforts so far. I'm sure Rebekah will be greatly missed by your whole group and we will not let her death be in vain.'

While this was all very comforting, I was very curious as to what the 'measures' were that would be put in place, and whether that would be detrimental to the research output. 'Measures' like that usually meant more paperwork, and less time in the lab.

Prof Gray stood and said, 'Thank you' and the Head left the room. As soon as the door closed behind her the noise level rose, everyone asking what the changes would be, and what was going on. Prof Gray called for silence and the group settled down.

'I want to add my sympathy to that of Margaret,' he said. 'We are all very saddened by the loss of Rebekah, and we want to make sure that something like this never happens again.'

'What did happen?' Wei called out.

'Well … I will say …'

'And what changes are there going to be? Will I still be able to do the digestions I need?' This was from Sophia.

'Let the man speak,' growled Robbie, and we were all quiet again.

'Rebekah died from an allergic reaction to latex gloves.'

'I knew it,' I whispered to myself.

'We knew she had this allergy, and I have talked to Robbie about the safeguards that had already been put in place to deal with that. We are working to understand how this dreadful accident could happen. One issue that we can see is that Rebekah was working after hours, alone in the lab, and therefore unable to get the help that she needed. And while there had been some safety measures in place, obviously they weren't enough to prevent this terrible … thing from happening.' Prof Gray's voice faltered.

Robbie sat beside me shaking his head. 'Shouldn't have happened at all,' he muttered. 'Don't see how it did.'

Prof Gray cleared his throat and pulled his shoulders back to start again.

'So as of now, there will be no after-hours work in the lab until after a full investigation has been made. And during work hours you are now required to have at least two people present in the laboratory for all experimental work.'

Groans and incredulous cries filled the room as this announcement was made.

'Even post-docs?' asked Mike. 'Surely this is just for students.'

'All of you. Everyone will be covered by this rule, at least until after we have talked with the WHS people.' Prof's tone indicated no possibility of compromise.

'Does it have to be two people in the lab? Can we just make sure there's someone in the office?' asked Tony, looking for a loophole.

Prof Gray looked at Robbie and Robbie shrugged.

'Yes, I think if there is someone in the office, that should be OK.'

'As long as they're not wearing the writing headphones,' Robbie said. I wondered what special thing the writing headphones were, but everyone else seemed to understand so I kept my questions for later.

'Fair enough,' said Tony. 'They'll need to be able to hear what's going on.'

'As investigations are ongoing, I trust that you'll give your full cooperation to police or university staff. And I encourage you to take advantage of the grief counselling that Margaret mentioned. Or come and talk with me about anything. My door is always open.'

I nodded but I noticed Wei giving Mike another meaningful glance. Maybe Prof Gray's door hadn't always been open in the past. Robbie had said that Mike was supposed to be the intermediary between the students and the professor. I couldn't see anyone going to Mike to talk about their issues with this though. He was not in any way the comforting shoulder to cry on.

'Any other questions?' Prof Gray asked, picking up his notebook and pen and preparing to leave.

'Are they sure it was an accident?' We all stared at Yusuf in surprise. What on earth was he suggesting? He looked surprised in turn.

'What? We all know how stressed she was. How hard she was working. How much pressure she was under. I'm just wondering if this was … well if she … you know.'

'That is completely unhelpful speculation,' Prof Gray growled. 'I'll thank you to not spread any rumours like that around the university. When we have more answers we will give them to you, but it will not make things any better for anyone to come up with any wild stories.'

Yusuf sat back in his seat and stared at the floor.

'Alright, everyone can get back to work. Mike I'll have you come and see me at 11 a.m. Alicia, I trust you're getting through everything OK despite this interruption?'

I nodded. Prof Gray obviously didn't want to talk with me at the moment, but it was kind of him to remember that I was a guest in this situation. He left the room and the conversations immediately started and bubbled around me. But I decided not to take part in any of them. It was time to get back to work, and I had plenty to do.

'Would it be alright to do the HF digestion today?' I asked Robbie.

'Sure, if you promise not to have a "terrible accident".' Robbie made the scare quotes in the air.

'It's not an accident if it's planned is it? I mean, an accident is accidental, you don't mean it to happen.'

'My point exactly,' said Yusuf butting into our conversation.

'Let it go,' growled Robbie.

'I just think … I mean … she was so down all the time.'

'I said, let it go!' Robbie stood up and leaned over Yusuf and the younger man shrank back into his seat.

'OK, OK.'

'Come on then,' Robbie gestured to me. 'If it's going to be HF we have some organising to do.'

I glanced back at Yusuf's glowering face as we left. If I knew anything about it, the kid had not let it go.

17

Time to don the white lab coat and the oversized safety glasses and to get some real lab work done.

I was surprised to feel little shimmers of excitement. It had been a while since I had worked on my own research. Lab life in Tasmania (working as a lab technician and helping out undergraduate students) had consisted of filling wash-bottles with acetone, and cleaning up the mess made by lazy people who were apparently not able even to wash up a beaker to the point where it was clean enough to be used again. Today, I would be working with my own samples, the catalysts that I had made previously, dissolving them in hydrofluoric acid (HF for short) for analysis, and also taking a fresh sample of the powder to check the surface area, all sorts of fun. Though, to be honest, I was feeling more than nervous about using HF. That acid was scary.

I will never forget that undergrad lecture where I had been told of the dangers of HF. 'You don't feel the burn,' said the imposing lecturer, leaning over the lectern for emphasis, so that a line of chalk dust formed on his black suit. 'But it penetrates your skin, and eats into your bones, leeching the calcium out. It takes a while to act, but once it starts taking the calcium out of the nervous system around your heart, that's the end of it. The end of you.' Scary, scary stuff.

So whenever someone worked with HF, major safety precautions were put in place. It may not have been the best time to do the digestion straight after what had happened to Rebekah, but then again, maybe it was. Maybe we were extra careful, keeping in mind the dreadful things that can happen when something goes wrong.

We set up the fume hood with warning signs, a bowl of calcium chloride solution to soak everything in, and a tube of calcium gluconate gel to spread on my skin if I managed to drop any HF on myself. I gloved up – nitrile gloves first, then big plastic gloves that reached to my elbows, then more nitrile on top. And Robbie agreed to be my right-hand man to keep an eye on things as I placed a few grams of my compounds into the plastic containers and added the HF to allow them to dissolve. The containers were plastic, because HF eats through glass. Every tool we used was plastic. Plastic pipettes, plastic containers, plastic stirrers. It felt very different to the glassware that we normally worked with, increasing my sense of danger. I worked carefully, and Robbie checked all my movements, every drop of clear fluid was accounted for. And after an hour or so of painstaking work, we were done.

'Phew. Time for morning tea, I think,' said Robbie.

I stripped off all the layers of gloves and dunked them into the calcium solution in the tub.

'Couldn't agree more.'

Robbie rang a little bell in the lab and everyone else downed tools too. It seemed that morning tea was a group activity. At least, most of the group was coming.

Sofia called out from her fume hood, 'I'm not quite finished yet. I just have to weigh out the hydroxide and put it in.'

'We'll see you down there,' said Wei.

'But …'

'Someone has to stay,' said Robbie. 'Have you forgotten already?'

I looked in the office to see if anyone was left behind. Yumi was sitting at her desk in the back of the office with bright red headphones on. The type you wear on a building site to block the noise and protect your ears. It was noisy in that office sitting as it was, right at the back of the lab. There was the noise from the extractor fans that ran day and night, the noise from the equipment pumping gas in and out of samples for surface area analysis, the various stirrer bars clinking against the side of the round-bottomed flasks. But I didn't think it was noisy enough to cause hearing damage. I wondered whether sound-cancelling headphones of that intensity were really necessary.

'Yumi's still there,' I said.

'Yumi? Nah, she's wearing the writing headphones,' Robbie replied.

'Writing headphones?' I definitely needed this term explained.

'They're like a big "Do Not Disturb" sign. They block the conversation, block the noise, and help you get your writing done. Wearing them is a sign that you're not to be interrupted.'

'Right,' I said. And the whole group of us stood around and stared at each other waiting to see who would blink first.

Eventually Sahar said, 'Oh alright. I'll stay. But I'm not staying every time. We're going to have to take turns at this.'

The rest of us nodded and traipsed out of the room, leaving safety glasses at the door. Sahar stood at the door, arms crossed, and stared at Sofia while she worked. This was going to be painful, I could tell. But I wasn't going to offer to stay. I really needed a cuppa after the HF work. My hands were trembling from the tension. I'd take a turn later on, maybe the next time someone needed babysitting.

18

'So we all have to be babysat now,' I explained to Martha over our now regular evening hot chocolate. 'It's like not being able to go into the kitchen and cook by yourself.'

'You poor things.'

'I know. The students are frustrated. Really frustrated. But what can you do?'

'It's better to be safe than sorry.' Martha nodded wisely.

'We really can't figure out how "the accident" happened at all.' I was now the one making scare quotes in the air. 'I've been thinking it over again and again. There is no reason why Rebekah should have come in contact with the gloves. It should not have happened. Robbie thinks so too. Yusuf thinks it's suicide.'

'Now, who is Yusuf again?'

'He's one of the students. He's from Malaysia. A really nice guy. Actually, you'd love him, he is so careful with what he wears – cufflinks, neatly pressed shirts. I think he'd wear a tie if it wasn't dangerous in the lab.'

'Oooh I do like it when the young people dress well.' Martha smoothed her hair with her hands and straightened her shirt.

I looked at her floral polyester shirt and pastel blue pants and nearly laughed. But then, I thought, she's looking after herself within her budget. And she's not wearing fluffy slippers or a stained apron or anything. In fact, I usually didn't think about what she was wearing at all – the life in her bright blue eyes was all I noticed.

But she'd gone away from the fashion talk, and back to the 'mystery' that she thought this death was.

'So this … Yusuf … he thinks Rebekah committed suicide?'

'He thinks so, but no one else does. They all just brushed it off when he brought it up.'

'How about you Luv? Do you think she could have done that?'

I took a few sips of my hot chocolate while I pondered. I hadn't spent much time with Rebekah, but …

'No. No I don't think so. She didn't look like it to me. She was stressed, but she was still intent on finishing her PhD. I think we can count that out.'

'So if it's not that, and it's not an accident … well, what's left, Luv?'

'Oh Martha.' I sighed.

'I'm just echoing what I'm hearing from you.' Martha's eyes twinkled.

But I sighed again.

'It must have been an accident. I mean, who would want to hurt Rebekah? I've had annoying office mates before. It happens, you deal with it.'

Martha nodded. I was sure she'd worked with all sorts of people during her life. And she definitely wasn't what you'd call a bitter person. She knew how to do inter-personal relationships.

But she wasn't going to let this go.

'Maybe someone from outside did it? Maybe she has a secret double life?'

'Martha,' I laughed. 'Rebekah couldn't even organise her first life, let alone another one.'

'Well, maybe that was why she was such a mess. Maybe leading a double life was getting too much for her. Maybe ...' Martha's voice fell low and ominous. 'Maybe she was into drugs.'

I looked at her and shook my head but she continued in a conspiratorial tone.

'Yes ... And she hadn't paid the dealer, and he came into the lab late at night when he knew she was working, and ...'

'We have swipe-cards,' I interrupted. 'We need them to get into the building after hours. If it comes to that, we need them to get into the lab at any time.'

'Ah.' Martha cheerfully took a sip of her chocolate. 'Well, that wipes that theory out, doesn't it?'

I thought about it.

'Not necessarily. I mean, my card took a couple of days to come, and while I was waiting, I either knocked on the lab door to get in, or I just waited until someone else opened the door.'

'So if it was someone she knew, she could let them in?'

'Yes, but if she was scared of them, she wouldn't do that, would she? And they would have to know to get into the building before closing and then hide somewhere until late. They would have had to know that she was in the lab working late. No, I don't think it was an outsider.'

'This is all very exciting, isn't it?' Martha smiled at me and I had to smile back. It was easy for her, though, she'd never met any of the people involved in this tragedy. For me, it was a little more complex, and a lot sadder. And for those people who knew Rebekah well? They'd be living with grief for the rest of their lives.

I suddenly realised that Rebekah must have a family somewhere. Parents, maybe siblings. Presumably they had been informed. What were they going through right now?

19

Friday morning, after chatting with all the oldies over breakfast and checking up on their various loved ones, I set off along Newtown Road on my normal walk to the university. I was so glad I was living only walking distance away. The short walk was a pleasant way to start the day, and much nicer than squashing myself onto a train or fighting the motion sickness that comes with a bus trip.

I heard the sound of drums as I neared the entrance to the university and I wondered what was going on. So many fun things happen on such a big university campus. Pop-up markets, or student union days with stalls and flash mobs and things. Or just students practising their circus skills in the little grassy nooks around the place – tying their slack lines to trees and doing acrobatics just for fun. The drums I was hearing could be an announcement of any of a number of fun things.

But I was to be disappointed.

As I rounded the last bend in the road I saw the owners of the drums. They were all dressed in matching purple T-shirts, and along with the drummers a whole lot of other people in purple were lined up at the entrance to the avenue. The banners they were waving told me that this was a protest by the union, the tertiary education union.

I didn't know what it was about, but I knew that I didn't want to get involved. But the chances of that were slim. I had to walk past them to get to the chemistry building and I knew they'd want me to join in.

I tried the 'put your head down and avoid eye contact' method, but a tall thickset redhead planted himself in front of me.

'Here, take one,' he said, waving a pamphlet under my nose.

'Ah…' was my nuanced response.

'It's disgusting! They should be ashamed of themselves.'

My curiosity got the better of me and I accepted the pamphlet from him, just to see what the fuss was about.

He let me walk past then, and I looked at the pamphlet as I walked along the avenue. I flinched. There on the purple sheet in front of me was a photo of Rebekah. Not a great photo, they probably used her student ID card, but it was definitely her. I frowned and read on to see what this was all about.

UNRELENTING PRESSURE CAUSES SUICIDE!

A PhD student has killed herself due to the pressures of university life. Students need a fair go! Scholarships force them to live below the poverty line. Fat-cat professors force them to work inhumane hours. Ban the slave trade of university research students!

'Well, that escalated quickly!' I thought. 'And who told them it was suicide? Yesterday we thought that her death was a horrible accident.'

I was approaching the chemistry building now and another crowd of students, staff, purple T-shirts and flyers was there to meet me. Big posters with Rebekah's photo on them were stuck next to the front door.

'Enough is enough!' they were shouting. 'Lower workloads now!'

It was going to be unpleasant if they kept this up all day. I wouldn't be heading out for coffee, that's for sure.

I waved my flyer and pushed through the crowd to get into the building. Hopefully that was the end of the purple T-shirts I would have to see. At least until the end of the day.

But that was not to be. In the office I saw another character in a purple T-shirt. It took me a bit to recognise him, the shirt being so different from his normal classy attire. It was Yusuf all dressed up and supporting the union. I wondered if I could avoid the conversation, then I realised I'd just be putting it off. I thought I'd get it over and done with.

'I didn't realise you were part of the union,' I said.

'Why wouldn't you be?' he answered. 'The way things are right now, you'd be crazy to try to go it alone. I guess you didn't hear about the whole pay issue that happened here last year?'

I shook my head. I was going to ask him to tell me, but I didn't have to.

'The uni stopped paying the casuals last year. No indication that they were doing anything. No explanation of why. But they didn't pay us for six weeks. Six weeks! I had rent to pay, I was getting really desperate. I depend on the undergraduate lab teaching to get through the year, you know?'

'Six weeks is a long time.' Despite myself I could really see his point of view. This was a bad situation if what he said was true. And it could easily be true.

'I don't think the uni were too worried about it. If the union hadn't got on to them I reckon we would have been stuffed.'

I nodded. I could see what he was saying. Big companies like the university can get away with murder if they are not held to account.

'Are you a union member?' he asked.

'I'm not even a proper employee at the moment,'

I said. But that was not excuse enough for Yusuf. He searched on his desk for an application form while I stood like a fly stuck on fly paper. Then I saw him move a pile of purple pamphlets, the same as the one I'd been given with Rebekah's photo on it, and I figured out how to deflect the conversation.

'How do they know that Rebekah's death was suicide?' I asked. 'I mean, I thought the official line was that it was an accident.'

'What? Oh.' Yusuf looked at the floor, his face flushing. 'Um …'

I couldn't believe it.

'You don't mean you told them that?'

'I might have.' He placed his lab book over the flyers, covering them up.

'But you don't know that's what happened, do you? … I mean, is it true? Do you know for sure?'

He turned and faced me defiantly.

'It's obvious to me. I don't know why it's not obvious to everyone. She's been working late evenings, weekends, all the time. I think the stress of it all just got to her. I mean, she's doing a PhD but that shouldn't mean 80-hour weeks. And we all know that the latex gloves are all locked up in the cupboard. There's no reason she should have touched one at all. So it *has* to be self-inflicted.'

'Yusuf, that's such a huge jump! You can't just go and tell everyone that she killed herself. It's not fair to her family, it's not fair to her friends. And it might not even be true.'

He looked down at the floor again, backing down before my attack.

'I didn't mean it to go that far,' he mumbled. 'I just went to the union office yesterday and chatted with Gordon, and next thing you know he's organised this huge protest.' Then he looked back up at me obstinately. 'People are working too hard here though. The pressure is huge. If Rebekah's death can help with that then she wouldn't have died in vain.'

He had a point. The union was important and it had such a vital role in keeping the university in check. Things were getting out of control with workloads and requirements, and the union was pushing back against the rampant commercialism. Still, I hoped that he hadn't muddied the waters with this protest.

We didn't really know why Rebekah died but I hoped that it wasn't suicide. Somehow I would feel so much more responsible if it was.

20

After my conversation with Yusuf I decided to stop thinking about Rebekah and instead pay attention to my seminar. I mean, this was the reason I was in Sydney. The seminar was my chance to impress people. I needed to show them that my research was special, ground-breaking, and that my teaching style was excellent. It was hard to break into this kind of position and I needed to be on top of my game. I needed to be ready for the interview too, of course. But preparing the seminar was more straightforward.

So I sat and polished and fiddled. Added new pictures, made sure the text was the right size and the right font. Used animations but only where they added to the story. Put together a script and then memorised it so it wouldn't sound like I was reading.

It wasn't exciting stuff, but eventually I had something that I was almost happy with.

There were gaps, of course. I still didn't have all the results from the analysis that I had been doing. The instruments were still running, and I was waiting in a queue for some analysis that I had sent off to another department. But I was sure they would all come in by Thursday. Well, I was nearly sure. They just had to, that was all there was to it. And I'd be able to put the details into the PowerPoint and give a beautiful seminar that was sure to get me a job. I repeated that sentence to myself, trying to build confidence that I just didn't feel.

Once I got the presentation to a place of near perfection, with just a few empty tables and spaces for graphs, I realised that just having a nice PowerPoint presentation on my computer wasn't enough. I needed to practise. I picked up my laptop and set out to find an empty lecture theatre. I was going to make the most of the unfair advantage of being in Sydney early. The other applicants could have come for two weeks if they had wanted to, I justified to myself, I was just doing the best I could to get a job.

Lecture Theatre One was occupied. The lecturer droning on about curly arrows – the very untechnical sounding technical term used to explain mechanisms in organic chemistry. Looking through the tiny square window in the door I figured there were hundreds of first-year students in there.

Lecture Theatre Two was empty, but it was also right next door to Theatre One and I didn't want to be seen practising by all the students as they filed out after their lecture. I walked upstairs to try one of the smaller theatres. They didn't have that imposing feel but they would still be a place where I could stand and deliver to an imaginary audience.

I tried the door to Theatre Four and it opened to reveal a compact room with a screen and about fifty tiered seats. This would work for my practice presentation. I set up my laptop on the bench in front of the screen and plugged it in, then squatted to look under the bench for buttons that would turn the projector on. Then I heard a noise that made me jump and hit my head on the bench.

'Ouch,' I said, maybe a little louder than was necessary.

'Sorry, I'm so sorry,' came a watery voice and I looked in that direction to see a bundle of misery in the back row.

'Yumi? What are you doing here?'

'I can go. I just …'

'No, no. You don't need to go, I mean, I can leave if you need me to. But … are you OK?'

I walked up the steps and squeezed myself along the row of seats to get to her in the corner.

Once again, that was the wrong question to ask. Her tears spilled over and I sat next to her, put my arm around her and waited for the flood to stop.

'It's so bad,' she finally said. 'I didn't know, it's so bad.'

'Start at the beginning and tell me all about it,' I said, trying to make my voice sound all motherly and warm, like Martha's.

'The police, they talk with me.'

'The police? Why?'

'They tell me I'm in trouble. They tell me … but I didn't know …' The tears started again but now I was confused. Why would someone as gentle and hardworking and, frankly, innocuous as Yumi, be in trouble with the police? I wished I could speak Japanese so that she could tell me her story more easily.

'Hang on – you're in trouble? What's going on?'

She sniffed and tried to get a hold of herself. 'I was there.'

'You were where?'

'I was there, in the office, when Rebekah …'

Was she telling me that she was present when Rebekah died? How could that have worked?

'How did they know you were there?'

'The card, the …' She made a movement with her hand.

'The swipe-card?'

'Exactly, yes. The records say I am there.'

'No,' I said flatly. 'That doesn't make sense. You would have heard something, seen something.'

She shook her head.

'No, that's it. I wear the …' Yumi cupped her ears with her hands. 'I am writing.'

'Ohhh.' It all became clear. 'You were wearing the writing headphones, the noise cancelling headphones. Writing at your desk in the corner of the office. Concentrating hard. And you didn't see anything or hear anything. Is that it?'

'The police … they …' She buried her face in her hands.

'But they have to believe you. They can ask anyone in the group about those headphones.'

She kept her head in her hands. I rubbed her shoulder, trying to give comfort, but thinking it through. I mean, this put the whole thing in a new light. If the police were asking questions like this, it might mean that Martha was actually right, that Rebekah's death was murder.

Although, they could just be trying to figure out how it all happened. Report for the coroner and all that. I pulled myself back into line. I needed to not get ahead of myself.

'Didn't you see Rebekah when you left the office?' I asked. She would have had to walk past the banks of fume hoods to get out of the office and go home. Unless she didn't go home. But surely Yumi wouldn't have stayed there all night.

And walking past the fume hoods, she must have seen Rebekah then. Anyone (even in the deepest thought) would have noticed someone slumped over, dead, as they walked out. I would have thought so, anyway.

'No,' she took her hands down from her face and looked at me. 'I went out the fire stairs. I was tired, not thinking. I just leave the quick way. Then, I remember, and I come back in the front door to sign the book. I didn't go out the lab.'

The after-hours book down near reception. You sign in if you're in the building after six, and you sign out when you leave. If there's a fire or something, the book is supposed to tell the emergency personnel who to look for. Apparently it also works (along with the electronic swipe-card records) to show the police who was around when someone died.

'The police can check that too,' I said. 'You told them, didn't you?' She nodded. 'Well then, that's good. That corroborates your story. I'm sure you'll be fine. You don't need to worry about the police.'

She shook her head and the tears came again.

'I don't mind police,' she said. 'I mind … I am there.' She looked at me with eyes wide and repeated the words more slowly. 'I am there.'

And finally I understood. She was Rebekah's friend, and Rebekah had died, right there in the lab, right under her nose. And she hadn't noticed. She could have done something to help, but she was so intent on writing her paper that she didn't realise what was going on. And she lost a friend. How horrible.

I didn't get any seminar practice that morning. I spent my time trying to comfort Yumi, and then finding a counsellor that she could talk with. And letting Prof Gray know that she was struggling. And then, finally, sitting in the café, sipping a coffee and wondering how Yumi would have coped with all this if I hadn't been there.

And wondering just how and why Rebekah had died.

21

'So you see,' I said to Martha over our evening cup of chocolate. 'I didn't get to practise after all. This Rebekah thing is really getting in the way of my plans for this fortnight.'

'This Rebekah thing,' she said, giving me a disciplinary tap on my shoulder. 'How dare she die like that? Right when you were trying for a job.'

I sighed.

'I know it's rude, but I didn't know her that well.'

'I know, and it's important, isn't it dear, that you get this job?'

'Well, it is really. Though maybe I'm asking too much. This is the first job I've applied for since Mum passed away.'

Martha nodded.

'It takes some time to work through grief enough to see any future. You had to give yourself time, now you're ready to take the next steps. Maybe the next step is getting the job, but maybe it was just a step of having enough energy to apply for one.'

Martha, she was such a warm friendly face, she lulled you into a sense of security, and then she said wise things like that.

'Perhaps you're right, perhaps applying is all that I'm meant to do. But I want to give it my best shot, and while I was happy to look after Yumi, I would have liked the time to practise the seminar.'

'Why don't you practise here, Luv?'

'Because I need a projector to plug my laptop into. It's not the same when you're talking to your computer screen. Nah, it's OK.'

'But we have one of those.'

I looked at her incredulously.

'Where?'

'Come with me.'

We went out of the stainless steel kitchen, through the pink dining room and into the dark hallway. Instead of going up the stairs, Martha pulled the back door open. I had seen the back courtyard through the dining room windows, but I hadn't realised that along a little veranda there was another wing of the building.

Martha pulled a bunch of keys out of her pocket and opened the door at the end of the veranda. When she switched on the light I saw a large rectangular room with a raised platform at one end. Black vinyl chairs were set out in rows and on the platform there was a lectern, a piano, and a few music stands scattered about.

'What's this?' I asked.

'We have church here on a Sunday. And healing services through the week. You didn't read the little pamphlet at the front door?'

I hadn't read any of the pamphlets at the front door. I guess I was too busy worrying what my room would be like on the first day, and since then I hadn't gone into the office.

'Now I'm not one for technical doodads, Luv, but I think you should be able to find something that works here.'

Martha led the way to a cupboard at the back of the room. And yes, we could find something there. There was a projector, even a screen – one of those free-standing ones, microphones, all the technical bits that I could ever need. I thought I'd keep it simple.

'If we just set up the projector so that it shines on the back wall, I could plug my computer into it and it would work brilliantly. Thanks Martha!' I started pulling the bits and pieces out. Checking if the power cord was there, and which cord I would be plugging into my computer.

'So when are we practising then?'

'We?' I was still absentmindedly pulling out and sorting the various black cords.

'You need an audience to practise to, don't you?'

I sat back on my heels and looked up at her.

'Oh no. You don't want to sit through that.'

'I think it would be very interesting,' she said. She crossed her arms. I had offended her. 'Do you think I'm not smart enough for your science? Is that it?'

'Oh no. No.' She'd got the wrong end of the stick. I tried to make it right. 'You can come if you like, I just thought it would be really boring for you. The students at uni do anything they can to get out of going to a seminar.'

'Well, I'm not a university student, and I'd like to hear it.'

'Sure, if that's what you want, I'm happy to have an audience. It would be good practice.'

'Shall we say, tomorrow at 10 a.m.?'

I was going to practise straight away, but then, it was getting quite late. Tomorrow would be good.

'Certainly. That would be wonderful,' I said with a grateful smile. Martha's return smile was huge. She was going to be so disappointed.

22

I didn't sleep well that night. I lay in bed worrying about the seminar and that had led to stressing about the job interview and those thoughts had brought me to thinking about the stress of the lecturing job itself. I stared at the ceiling, tying myself up in knots trying to figure out if I really wanted to get this position, if I wanted to move back to this big city from my little town in Tasmania, if I needed the stress and workload and everything that went with it. But then, I needed to work somewhere, and I was a scientist, and ... my thoughts went around and around in circles.

I woke feeling worse for wear, and decided that a double-shot latte would set me up better for the seminar practice than a bowl of cornflakes, and that a walk along the street wouldn't hurt either.

At 10 a.m. I pushed open the door to the 'church room' and the sound of friendly chatting made me jump. It looked like I wouldn't be able to practise my talk after all. Martha mustn't have known about this meeting. Whatever it was for.

I turned to leave, hoping I hadn't been too much of a distraction when Martha saw me and waved enthusiastically.

'You're here!' she said. 'We're all ready for you.'

I rushed over, grabbed her by the arm and pulled her to the back corner of the room.

'What have you done?' I hissed.

'I told you, you need an audience to practise to. Plus all of us want to hear about what you do.'

I looked around at the lovely grey-haired audience. They looked excited, anticipating who knows what. Oh, this was not going to be good. I would bore them all to tears.

'I hope you don't regret this,' I groaned.

Then I put on my best performance smile and turned to the 'audience'.

'Hello everyone, thank you for coming to hear me this morning,' I said, enunciating clearly and speaking loudly. 'If I was intending to give a seminar for you all, this is probably not the one I'd choose and I hope you don't find what I'm saying to be too boring. But I really appreciate you giving your time to listen to me. There are going to be a few gaps that I'm hoping to fill in with this week's work, but you should get the gist, anyway.'

Everyone clapped enthusiastically. I guess that this was a different thing in their difficult lives. A change of pace. An entertainment. Anyway, I decided to give it a good go.

I saw just about everyone's eyes glaze over after the first few minutes of my talk. I could have told them this would happen. The seminar was deep chemistry, lots of facts and figures and terminology they had never heard before. Zeolites, protonation, catalysis, yields and turnover numbers. Not the most riveting of seminars, even if you're a chemist yourself. I was tempted to rush it, to skip things. But then, this was my practice for the real thing. I needed to practise properly. And in the end I didn't do too badly. Only one lady fell asleep, her head dropping forward to her chest. And there was one man who sat bolt upright and with bright eyes through the whole talk. He looked like he might have even been enjoying it.

When I finished my last slide, he started the clapping. And the sleeping woman woke up and joined in with the applause.

'Thank you so much,' I said. 'Are there any questions?'

The room filled with silence. As I looked out at the blank stares in front of me I felt a sense of déjà vu. Oh yes, it had been just like this when I'd been the first presenter at a symposium the day after the conference dinner. The audience on that occasion were too hungover to care about the talk. At least these lovely people cared, even if they struggled to understand.

There was no point in waiting for questions. There were no questions coming. I broke the silence.

'Thanks so much everyone again for listening. I really appreciate it.'

They slowly pulled themselves out of their seats, groaning and stretching, and the room filled again with friendly chatter as they filed out the door.

'Wasn't that lovely?' I heard. And, 'So much information she has in her head.'

I felt for them. What a boring half hour it had been.

Then the bright-eyed gentleman came and shook my hand.

'That was a very interesting talk indeed,' he said. 'I enjoyed that immensely.'

'Thank you,' I responded with a smile. 'Are you a scientist?'

'Oh, it wasn't my area at all, I'm a physicist, but I enjoyed the brain food nevertheless. I haven't been to a talk for a while, not since my wife became ill. I've missed them.'

'I'm sure. I hope your wife is getting better?' I thought that was the polite thing to say. But he shook his head.

'I'm afraid it's not long now.'

I didn't know what to say. And he generously filled my awkward silence.

'Anyway, it was a good talk. Well done. I hope you are able to fill the holes.'

That was also a difficult subject. I hadn't expected a professional to be listening to my practice.

'Yes, I don't normally give an incomplete talk. I hope I can fill them in too.'

We said our goodbyes, and that left myself and Martha in the room. While we packed up the cords she also let me know what she thought of my talk.

'That was amazing, Luv,' she gushed. 'You just went on and on. I couldn't believe how much you had to say.'

'How much did you understand?' I asked.

'Oh, nothing at all,' she said with a large smile. 'But I was very impressed, all the same! Everyone was, you could tell.'

'Well, it was really lovely of everyone to come and hear me. I'm sure I'm much better prepared for Thursday's seminar from today.'

'You'd better take yourself off to work and get those last few numbers for your tables. I'll finish off here.'

I hoped I could get those numbers too. If Martha, and that lovely gentleman who both knew nothing about the subject matter were aware of the holes, then the chemistry professors were sure to be super-aware. If the practice had shown me nothing else, it had shown me the importance of full tables. If I couldn't get the results I needed I'd have a lot of rewriting to do.

23

'Good morning everyone,' said Prof Gray.

It was a quiet Monday morning, and most of us in the office were sitting at our desks, catching up on email and planning the day's work.

I looked up to see Prof Gray standing at the entrance to the office, near the yellow cupboards. Next to him stood a middle-aged woman with long blonde hair and a thin, downturned mouth that was outlined in bright red lipstick. She wore a black shirt over white pants, and a small cross hung on a thin silver chain around her neck. She was holding herself carefully as if she was exerting every ounce of her energy to keep herself together. She was on the verge of shattering into a million pieces.

'Everyone, this is Sheila, Rebekah's mother. She's here to pick up Rebekah's personal effects from her desk. I hope you will all make her feel welcome.'

A chorus of subdued hellos followed his announcement. As Rebekah's desk was next to mine, I stood and welcomed her properly.

'Her desk is just here. I'm sorry we haven't gone through it yet and cleaned it up.'

'No, no,' she said in a broken voice. 'It's not your responsibility. I just … I thought I'd check …'

'Of course, you want everything that's meaningful to you. Here, let me help.'

I picked up some of the print-outs of journal articles and the piles of student lab books and piled them onto my desk so that Sheila could get through to the items that would mean more to her. She sorted through the mess of scraps of paper to find notebooks and pens, a framed photo of the family, the calculator with Rebekah's name painted on the lid in White-out, the bobble-head figurines, and the necklace that had been dropped into the desk drawer. All the bits and pieces that make up a life.

As we worked, we unearthed a half-eaten muesli bar, and an open box of crackers. And even the peel of a banana. I put the banana peel in the bin as quickly as possible, but amazingly it was this rubbish that triggered Sheila's emotions. Her tears welled and she pulled a handkerchief out of her pocket to dab at her eyes.

'I'm sorry, it's just … she was always so messy. It's a silly thing, but the banana peel … well, it just means more to me than these papers and notes. She was always in a muddle, always so disorganised. It is crazy to me that I won't be cleaning up her mess anymore. Not here, not at home.'

The tears came thick and fast.

'Come on,' I said. 'Let's get out of here and go for a walk. This will wait.'

She sniffed and nodded and we escaped down the fire stairs.

Just below the Camperdown campus of the Sydney University is Victoria Park. It's a beautiful oasis of green in the middle of the busy streets and shopping malls. Sheila and I walked down the grand sandstone steps of the uni and followed the path beneath the trees, hearing the excited shouts of children splashing in the swimming pool to our right, smiling at the couples cuddling on the park benches and the family groups leaving their picnic rugs to feed their leftover sandwiches to the ducks on the pond.

Slowly the colour returned to Sheila's face, and her tears dried up. We walked over the white-railed bridge, enjoying the water feature in the centre of the pond. Then we found our own park bench and sat to watch the children climbing on the play equipment.

I was quite happy to just sit there silently, if that was what Sheila wanted. But she started to tell me about Rebekah, and I realised that she needed someone to offload to.

'She didn't really want to come here, you know. I knew that she was bright, and that she could do it. But this wasn't her plan. She was quite happy to stay in Armidale, maybe go to uni there, get the training she needed to take over the property when her dad was ready to retire. If I'd known, maybe I wouldn't have ...' her voice trailed off.

'How did you convince her to come?'

The tears came again, and I waited for her to get whatever it was off her chest.

'We looked like such a normal family, but we weren't really. And I thought that … he was so angry, you know? We were trying to hide it, trying to put up with it. But I thought that she would be safer here. So when I heard about the scholarship … I just thought it would be better, you know?'

'You weren't to know. And any mother would do that. If her daughter could get a scholarship. I mean, Rebekah getting that scholarship, that meant she belonged here, didn't it?'

I expected my words to be comforting, but Sheila shook her head and cried even more. I put my arm around her and made soothing noises.

'You weren't to know,' I said. 'No one could have foreseen this.'

After a few minutes she dried her eyes, blew her nose, and straightened her shoulders.

'You're right,' she said. 'I wasn't to know. I did what I thought was right.' She wiped her eyes again. 'And maybe it was better for her here. At least she wasn't at home with him for the last few years. It had to have been better here.'

'Are you still with him?' I asked. She shook her head and stared unseeingly at the playground.

'No. No. I finally left last year. With Rebekah safely here, I realised that I could get out by myself. It was the hardest thing I've ever done, but I got out.

I got her into Sydney University, and I got myself away from him.'

She stared out at the playground again.

'I thought that meant that she was safe. She was supposed to be safe.' Her voice was so low that I could barely hear it.

We sat there in silence for a little while and then she shook herself and stood up.

'Thank you for that. That's just what I needed. But we can't sit here forever. I need to pack up the desk, and you, I'm sure, have heaps of work to do.'

'I'm happy to take the time that you need.' I really was happy. I mean, I had things to do, for sure, but people are more important, aren't they? But Sheila was determined.

'No, don't be ridiculous. I shouldn't be keeping you from your job. Let's get on with this.' She brushed the dust off her white pants and we walked together back up to the university campus.

In the office she turned to me, 'You've been very kind, but I'm sure I can manage from here. I've taken up a lot of your time. I won't take up anymore.'

'If you're sure …' I said.

'I'm sure.' Her voice was firm and she seemed to have control of her tears so I left her to it as she sorted through the remaining mess and placed the important things into a cardboard box.

I got on with my own writing, squeezed over to the side of my desk by the pile of Rebekah's paperwork.

I got a little bit done, but soon I became aware of Sheila opening each of the drawers in turn, sifting through things in the cardboard box, and looking behind piles and under the desk.

'What's up?' I asked.

'Sorry, I didn't want to bother you again, but do you have Rebekah's phone on your desk? You didn't pick it up with the papers did you?'

'Noooo,' I said slowly. I picked up the papers and looked again. 'No, it's not here. You don't have it?'

'No, it's not with her gear. And her epipen isn't here either. It's strange. I thought it would all be here.'

I stood up and called out to the room. 'Has anyone seen Rebekah's phone or epipen?'

There was a general chorus of negatives.

'We can't find them on her desk.'

'The phone shouldn't be hard to lose,' Robbie said. 'It was bright pink. I'll go have a look in the lab.'

'Thank you,' said Sheila. 'I guess they could be at her apartment. I just would have thought …'

I would have thought so too. Everyone took their phones everywhere with them, and Rebekah had told me just the other day that the epipen was in her desk drawer. It was very strange.

Robbie walked back in with his hands outstretched to show that he hadn't had any luck.

Sheila took a deep breath.

'Ah well. Can't have everything,' she said. 'If you find it, please let me know?'

'Of course.'

'I think that's probably everything then,' she said and picked up the cardboard box.

'I'll see you out,' said Robbie, taking it from her. He could be a gentleman when he wanted to.

I waited until Sheila was safely out of the lab, then I lifted up the heavy pile of paper and dumped it back onto Rebekah's desk. Someone would have to go through that sometime, but it didn't have to be me. I needed to get some of my own work done.

24

'No phone and no epipen, hey?' Martha and I were back to drinking our hot chocolates, and Martha was back to her sleuthing.

'They're probably at her apartment. She probably forgot to bring them in that day. She was a contestant for the "World's Worst Organised Person" award. If not a winner.'

'Or maybe the police took them.'

'Maybe.' I was doubtful. 'Why do you think they would need her phone?'

'The killer could have rung her and got her to let him in to the building.'

Martha had an answer for everything. And I had a question to go with her every answer.

'Right. And why would she do that?'

'Well, she knew him. Right?'

'But …'

Martha suddenly slapped the stainless steel bench causing the whole thing to wobble.

'You know Luv, I've got it. I know who killed her.'

'Oh Martha …' I got off the stool and went to the sink to find a cloth to clean up the spilt hot chocolate. Martha swivelled around on her stool to face me, her eyes very bright.

'It's right there in front of us. Can't you see it?

Come on Luv, guess.'

'Well, it's definitely not Sheila.' I couldn't think who else it could be, but Martha was too excited to let me go through the list of possible suspects.

'No, not her, not the mother. The father.'

'The father?' I rinsed the cloth in the sink.

'Rebekah's father. He was a bad man. He had a temper. His wife left him. He came to talk to Rebekah and he killed her.'

I thought about that as I sat back down and sipped my drink. There was merit in the idea. This man was abusive, and controlling. He didn't really want Rebekah to leave home, but Sheila organised for Rebekah to leave in a way that he couldn't stand up to. He could have sat and stewed and then come to Sydney and …

'It's a long drive to stay angry for. Hours and hours. Why would he do that?'

'To get back at his wife for leaving.'

'Why not just find his wife in his home town and kill her?'

'Maybe he's going to do that next.'

25

'Yumi, when you talked with the police, who did you talk to?'

Yumi pursed her lips, thinking hard.

'I think, Bill? Let me think. I don't …'

'If you can't remember, don't worry, it's OK.'

I had hoped that she'd remember. If I was going to talk to the police about Martha's crazy ideas it would be easier if I knew a name to ask for. But instead I would have to go to the local station and just ask. It would be a bit embarrassing and I wasn't sure if they'd take me seriously, but you have to do what you have to do. And just in case Martha was anywhere near right, I thought that this was what I had to do.

'Hang on.' Yumi opened her cute pink Minnie Mouse purse and searched in it. 'It's here somewhere. Ha!'

She pulled out a business card.

'Here you go. The man, he give me this.'

'Detective Sergeant William Severn', the card read. And a phone number and everything. That was exactly what I needed.

'Thanks! Can I take this?'

'Sure.' Yumi nodded enthusiastically. And then she asked me the question I was hoping to avoid.

'Why do you need it?'

Did I go into all of Martha's ideas about murder and suspects? Did I talk about Sheila's confession of an abusive husband and father? Or …

'I just want to make sure he knows that we couldn't find Rebekah's phone.' That was believable enough, wasn't it? It seemed to be. Yumi was satisfied. But she had something more to ask.

'Maybe, if you talk to him, can you tell him something?'

'A message from you?

'Yes, I remembered something. I wasn't sure to tell but maybe you can tell, if you are already talking.'

That was interesting.

'Sure. I can tell him.'

Yumi looked around the office. Then she motioned for us to go out to the fire stairs. So this was a secret thing, was it?

'I remembered a thing. On the night that …'

'The night Rebekah died.' She just didn't seem to be able to say it, so I helped her out.

'Yes, early that night I am in the lab, just finishing, and I hear a knock.'

'You let someone into the lab?' This could be really important information. Was it Rebekah's dad that Yumi let in? But I was to be disappointed. It was nothing that exciting.

'Yes, just Mike. He say he forgot his swipe-card on his desk. But then he came in, and he work for a while. I start writing, put the headphones on. I think that he went, but I don't know when. And he might see something that could help police.'

'Did you tell him to talk with the police?'

'I didn't talk to Mike. He … he … I can't tell him to do it.'

'I'm sure you could tell him. I'm sure he'd want to be helpful to police.'

'You can tell him,' Yumi said brightly. 'But maybe not say I told you.'

I realised what was going on. Mike was the boss. Yumi didn't want to be seen to be telling the boss what to do. She didn't think it was her place to tell Mike anything. But she thought I could, or the police could, or pretty much anyone other than her. She just didn't want to rock the boat.

And come to think of it, I didn't really want to rock the boat either. Going to Mike and saying, 'you were there when Rebekah died' was pretty much the same as saying, 'you killed her, didn't you?' And that was just stupid.

He probably came into the lab, went to his desk and picked up his keys and card, and then fiddled around a bit before leaving again. Probably hours before Rebekah got into trouble. Probably didn't have anything to do with anything.

Would I even tell the police? I remember the response I had in previous investigations, giving this kind of tangential information. Nate, who knew me, who was my friend, he didn't like hearing this kind of thing from me. How was a complete stranger going to take it? Maybe I'd just let it go. It was going to be embarrassing enough telling them about Rebekah's dad.

I just about decided to drop it.

But then I decided that I could help Yumi out. I was going to talk with the police anyway. I was already going to be embarrassed. I would ring this detective and see what he was like. And I'd let him know all the information that I knew.

26

'Hello, Bill Severn speaking.'

It was an older man's voice. Gruff, but friendly. I introduced myself and explained that I had some information that he might be interested in, pertaining to the death of Rebekah. I was ready to tell him everything over the phone but he wasn't keen to do that.

'I'll come down to the café just over the way from your building. We can meet there and you can tell me your information.'

'Sure,' I said. 'I have short, black hair and I'm wearing jeans and a forest-green t-shirt.' In other words, I look similar to any uni student, but I couldn't think of an outstanding characteristic that would define me. I'm not the sort for big creative statements – no floppy hats or big jewellery.

'I'll find you,' the gruff voice responded. 'I'll see you there in about ten minutes.'

I expected Detective Sergeant William, or Bill as he obviously liked to be called, to be wearing police gear. But he wore chinos and a blue open-necked shirt with the sleeves rolled up. He was a short, stocky man with a furrowed face, salt-and-pepper hair and a short beard. We sat at a table and ordered coffee. He took a flat white. Nothing fancy. I don't think there was anything fancy at all about Bill, instead he looked dependable. Really trustworthy.

That was probably how he got perps to open up to him – he looked like the kind of person you'd be happy to tell your life story to. He could have made a mint working in journalism, I thought. But that trustworthy face was just as useful to him working as a detective.

'Now, what information do you have for me?' he asked.

'Well, there's two things.' I felt my stomach contract, I was so nervous. What if he laughed me out of the place? What if I was totally wasting his time? What if he just got annoyed with Martha and me for chatting about this whole thing in the first place?

I took a deep breath and continued.

'I was talking to Rebekah's mum the other day and she told me that her marriage was … was a violent one. That Rebekah had come here to Sydney to get away from her father. And I wondered if you had looked into him, her father that is, as a possible … well … suspect?'

Bill looked at me with a half-smile.

'Who says that we are looking for suspects?'

There it was.

'Ah, well, no-one really.' I couldn't meet his eyes. The waiter brought our coffees and placed them on the table and I used that time to give me space to think. I wished the ground would swallow me up. But then, I'd made the date, I'd told Yumi that I'd say something. It was time to just go ahead and blurt it all out. So I took a sip of my coffee to give me confidence, and made the jump.

'Look, I'm trying not to be crazy or an amateur detective,' I said.

Bill raised an eyebrow, but I was on a roll now.

'But this whole situation seems really weird to me. It's weird that Rebekah died at all. It's weird that she died from contact with gloves she knew she was allergic to. That … you know … that her phone and epipen are missing from her desk. And she told me she kept an epipen in her desk. And everything.'

I took another sip of my coffee. Bill put his down on the table with a sigh.

'So, the phone and the epipen are missing. Is that the other thing you had to tell me?'

'You didn't know that? I was sure Sheila would have told you that.' I didn't mean to blurt that out. What must he be thinking now? I couldn't tell from his totally closed face and little half-smile.

'I'm not saying we didn't know, I'm just asking if that's what you had to tell me?' Bill was all pleasant and friendly, but his face didn't give anything away. I didn't know what to think. Should I keep going? I'd promised Yumi, so I took a deep breath and kept going.

'No, that wasn't the other thing.'

'So?' he asked.

'So, the other thing was something that Yumi asked me to tell you. Do you remember Yumi?' He nodded. 'She said that Mike had also come in that evening. He had knocked on the door because he had left his swipe-card in the office. She had let him in, and then got on with her writing. With the headphones on. I can vouch for those headphones, by the way, when she's writing with them on she doesn't notice anything that's happening around her at all. She is totally focussed. She puts her head down and sees nothing, hears nothing, it's like she's in a different world.'

'Thank you, but we did listen to Yumi when she told us. You don't need to worry. We're just trying to figure out what happened. We're not going to arrest someone just because they happened to be there.'

I nodded.

'So, that's it? You wanted to tell me that Yumi wasn't involved?'

'And that maybe Mike saw something before he left. Maybe he has part of the puzzle.'

'OK. Thank you for meeting with me.' Bill spoke evenly, like a school principal talking with a student. 'I agree with you that we don't want anyone jumping to conclusions or even talking too much about this. It would not be helpful to any of Rebekah's family to have wild rumours circulating.'

'Oh, no. I totally understand,'

I did too. I didn't want to be making things more difficult for poor Sheila.

'Great. Thanks again for the information.' Bill looked at his empty cup, and finally there was some emotion on his face. I wished I had enough money to donate a decent coffee machine to the police station. It looked like that was all Bill really cared about. But the cup was empty and he stood to leave.

'If I need you to do anything more formal I will definitely let you know. And you obviously have my number if there is anything else that you wish to tell me.'

And that was that.

But at least I'd been heard. I'd told him what I was thinking. And maybe now I could get the whole thing out of my head, and just concentrate on getting myself a job. That's what I was here for, the seminar and interview day was looming. I had experimental results to collect and make sense of and put into my talk. I had to think hard about what I was going to answer for such questions as, 'What is your philosophy of teaching?' and 'Where do you see yourself in five years' time?'

Rebekah had died. It was shocking. It was tragic. But it wasn't really my problem. Getting myself a job – now that was.

27

I stepped out of the café into the beautiful sunshine. The weather, the gorgeously warm winter weather. It was probably blowing sideways sleet down in Hobart and it was so beautifully sunny here with a light cool breeze to stop it from being overpoweringly warm. I couldn't go back inside. Not yet. Not to the humming of the fume hoods and the bright artificial fluorescent lights. I would go down to the park and have a walk first. Clear my head. Get myself right into the job-hunting zone.

OK, so I was just procrastinating, but it really was a beautiful day.

I did a circuit of the park. Down the wide sandstone steps and past the luscious green garden beds. I turned right at the bottom of the steps and walked along the grass past the swimming pool as far as the road that bordered the park on the southern side. Then along the road, past the play equipment and back over the pond using the beautiful white bridge and up the hill. By the time I got back to the steps I was well and truly refreshed. I had remembered about five things I needed to do, or really, five things I should have done already. I realised that I had been wasting my time thinking about Rebekah, I needed to get on with it.

I picked up my pace. It was time to be in at the office, doing the work.

As I walked briskly up the steps, a well-dressed woman in her late twenties offered me a business card. I took it, said 'thanks' and kept going. I tucked it into my pocket. I wasn't going to be sidelined by conversation or sales talk for whatever it was she was selling. It was time to work.

But when I sat down at my desk, the card in my pocket dug into my stomach. I pulled it out and looked at it. The list of things to do receded again as the card caught my attention.

'Essays and More' it said in dark blue writing on the pale blue background. Then there was a website. And then:

'Are you worried about your assignment? We provide the best quality essay writing service!'

Hang on, what was this? Essay writing?

I looked at the card more closely. Yes, it was an advertisement for an essay writing service. If you told them when your assignment was due, and gave them an indication of your writing style, they would write your essay for you.

I was pretty impressed by the nerve of the lady handing these out right at the doorway of the university. I mean, that was where you were going to get your students, sure. But it was also where the staff would find you.

Surely this was illegal?

And the best thing about the card was that it had a typo in the word 'editing'. So it was hardly a high-class cheating service. That particular typo made me laugh out loud; I wondered who could be taken in enough to use a service like this.

28

As I chuckled away, Robbie walked into the office past the yellow cupboards, pulling his lab coat off.

'Something funny?' he asked.

'Oh my goodness, it's hilarious.' I said. 'I got handed this card as I walked up the Victoria Park steps. The cheek of it. I can't get over it. It looks like I can come here and do a degree and not do any work – this group will do it all for me.'

Robbie took the card and had a close look at it.

'Can you see the typo?' I asked. '"Editiors" it says, like I'm going to let them anywhere near my work.'

'There's more than one typo. "Provide evidences", it says. Tell us the "due data"? Idiots.' He handed the card back to me and I looked at it again.

'Your whole degree – outsourced. What a plan.'

'Can't see it working for chemistry – maybe a whole arts degree could be outsourced though.'

Our sarcasm filtered through to Tony, who spun his chair around to face me.

'Show me that!' He snatched the card out of my hand and glared at it.

'What? Hey!' I said as he ripped the card in half. 'What's your problem? It's just a bit of a laugh.'

'No. No it's not,' he said, a muscle twitching in his jaw. 'It's not funny at all. I should tell the police.'

'But, Tony, surely offering help to students is not a criminal act.' I said. 'I mean, if someone cheats and pays these guys and you can catch them in the act, then the uni could throw them out. But you can't do anything about people offering an editing service. And a crap editing service, at that.'

'Yeah, come on man, settle. It's not that important.' Robbie tried to calm him down. But Tony stood up and roared in Robbie's face.

'Not that important? Can't you see that it devalues everything we do here? This is Sydney University! It's the best uni in the country. And you want people to get through because they pay someone to do their work? It makes a mockery of all our hard work! It makes our degrees mean nothing!' Tony slammed the yellow cupboard with his fist. 'It shouldn't be allowed. You know it. It's like … it's like what Rebekah did. It just makes everything we work for a sham!' He looked like he was about to hit the cupboard again, then he must have thought better of it because he turned abruptly and walked out the door to the fire stairs. Robbie and I stared at each other.

I turned to look around the office. Mike was halfway out of his chair, Yumi, for once not wearing the headphones, was watching with large, worried eyes. Sofia absentmindedly nibbled the end of her ponytail until she saw me watching, and then swished it back disdainfully.

'Well, he was a bit … um … shall we say, worried?' Robbie asked to break the tension.

'Concerned, maybe,' I said.

'Absolutely troppo, maybe.' Robbie looked over at the door with raised eyebrows.

'Do you think he's going to hurt anyone? Should we follow him?' I asked.

'Do you want to follow him?' asked Robbie.

'Ah, no, maybe it's better to let him calm down a bit.'

This seemed like wisdom to all of the office-mates and gradually we relaxed and went back to our work. Tony would be fine. He was an adult, he knew how to behave.

Something was bugging me though, and after a few minutes I walked to Robbie's desk to quietly ask him about it.

'Do you know what he meant about Rebekah?'

'No. I have no idea,' said Robbie, and not nearly as quietly as me. 'They came from the same town, you know. From Armidale. Maybe it was something she did in high school, or something like that.'

'What a coincidence – them coming from the same place. It's a fairly small place too.'

'Yeah, there's this scholarship drive from Sydney Uni for kids in the outback, and those two were some of the winners that year. Last year? The year before? Yeah, that's it. Two years ago. Most of the time people go to arts and so on, but you know how these things happen, how they go in waves? It was Armidale's turn to provide scientific geniuses.'

'Still, such a small town, in such a big country.'

Robbie nodded.

'I think that Tony's always been jealous of Rebekah. There was that rivalry aspect, you know? He was so sure he was better than her, but there they were, winning the same scholarship.'

'Maybe that's what he was getting at?'

'Maybe. But who cares? Getting the scholarship just gets you here. You have to put the work in to get anywhere after that. And Tony, well you saw his talk at group meeting. He's a bit of a genius. Rebekah … not so much. I don't want to speak ill of the dead, but, really, she didn't have a lot going for her in the smarts department.'

Robbie finished whatever he was typing into his computer, put his white coat back on, and headed back to the lab. Sometimes I envied him his ability to not worry.

29

That afternoon, I was working in the lab, trying to carefully measure 100 mg of my catalyst into the narrow-necked flask used for BET analysis. My catalyst is a microporous powder. It looks a bit like finely powdered salt or sand, but inside each grain are lots and lots of teeny tiny holes and tunnels. It's meant to be like that. The holes and tunnels, the pores, give a greater surface area where the molecules can go and react.

The thing is, scientists working with these kinds of catalysts want to know just how much surface area there is. And the way to find that out is to do BET analysis. You put a very small amount of catalyst into a glass container that has a long, skinny neck and a little bulb at the end. (How much of the powder do you put in? Well, the instructions helpfully say to add enough to be able to do the analysis, but not too much. Clear? I thought not, but that's what you get.) You need to measure the amount you put in, to the nearest 0.00001 gram. Everything has to stay clean and dry. So dry that even fingerprints are a problem, so there are some cotton gloves next to the instrument to stop your sweaty hands from doing damage.

After that tricky bit has been done, and you've recorded the mass (making sure that no stray breezes change the measurement) then you attach the glass flask to the measuring instrument and line up a liquid nitrogen container underneath your sample so that the instrument can lift it up to cool your sample, or drop it when your sample needs to heat up a bit.

That's another tricky bit. Liquid nitrogen is cold. Like very cold. Like minus two hundred degrees Celsius. So pouring that in to the container can be a bit scary. It's not too bad, you just have to be careful. It evaporates really quickly if you spill it, and makes a nice fog in the air around your feet. You can feel like a rock star for about two seconds.

Anyway, sample in place, liquid nitrogen container in place, everything is ready to go.

Then, you press play and the instrument dries every bit of water out of your sample under vacuum, and then fills it with gaseous nitrogen, and then measures the volume and calculates the surface area.

It's tricky stuff, and quite delicate. Especially the bit where you're weighing out a fly-away white powder that you've already got as dry and fluffy as you can, and then a really loud Bollywood ring tone blares out at you and gives you a fright and you drop the white powder all over the desk.

Well, that's what I found anyway.

'Whose blasted phone is that?' I yelled.

Yes, I was less than pleased. I didn't have time to waste, and I didn't really have catalyst to waste either.

Yumi walked into the lab. Her face as pale as if she had seen a ghost.

'It's Rebekah's,' she said.

'Sorry?' I was a little confused.

'Rebekah's phone. That is her phone sound.'

Forgetting all about my sample I followed the noise to the big black plastic rubbish bin under the sink. There, amidst all the paper towel and plastic waste was a bright pink mobile phone.

I picked the phone up and looked at it. Should I answer? But the phone stopped ringing. Yumi looked at it over my shoulder.

'What's it doing in the bin?' she asked.

'Someone must have put it there,' I said.

'Who would do that?'

It occurred to me that a person who would throw out Rebekah's phone would be a person who had something to hide. Why else would it be in the bin? I needed to get this phone to Bill. I was suddenly glad I was still wearing the cotton gloves and hadn't left any fingerprints on the phone.

'I don't know who would throw it out,' I said to Yumi. 'But I think I know what we should do with it. She'll be right, leave it with me.'

Yumi seemed to be comforted by that, happy to head back to her desk. And I made myself go back to the BET machine, use a nice soft paintbrush to clean away the white dust I'd spread around, and finish weighing and setting up my catalyst.

Then, careful to not leave my fingerprints on the phone, I found a plastic bag to put it in, took off my lab coat and the gloves, and hurried down to the café to ring Bill.

He told me he'd be around in ten minutes. The lure of the coffee was too strong for him to resist, as I had hoped.

I pulled the phone out of my pocket in its plastic bag and, out of habit, pressed the button to light up the screen. And the screen filled up with information.

The top line on the screen was the number that the latest call was from. The call that alerted me to the phone in the first place. But unhelpfully there was just a number, not a name. I guessed that meant that the call wasn't from anyone in her contacts. It didn't come from her father, or her mother, or any other named person. Well, it was probably just a travel agent, or a scammer, or some charity looking for donations.

But under that number there were some texts. And they were named.

The latest texts on Rebekah's phone came from Tony.

I checked the date.

Tony had been texting Rebekah on the night she died, asking her to meet with him here, at the very café I was sitting in – to discuss something!

I dropped the phone on the table when I saw that. Then fumbled and caught it as it bounced towards the floor. I couldn't believe what I was seeing. Had I really stumbled across evidence pointing to a murderer?

The noise from the café, the sights and sounds, all became dim as I imagined what might have happened the night that Rebekah died.

Tony texted Rebekah, and she met with him, maybe at a table like this one right at the back.

No, that couldn't be right. I pressed the button and looked at the text again. Tony had said 'tonight, at 7' and this place wasn't open past 4 p.m. So they couldn't have come inside to talk. They would have been sitting at one of the metal picnic tables outside. It would have been fairly dark, and they would have been talking in the dim evening light, faces lit by the streetlights from the Avenue.

They would have talked about whatever it was that he had been yelling about in the lab earlier today. That thing that had slipped out when he was upset about the business card. I'm sure the conversation got heated very quickly. Tony would have lost his temper, just like he had this morning. Maybe he was slapping the table, maybe he was waving his fist at her.

I'm sure she was scared. I'm sure his intimidating manner brought back all sorts of memories of a violent father. She would have run away, trying to get back to a place where she felt safe. But he would have followed her back to the chemistry building.

She would have used her swipe-card to open the building door and the lab door, and he would have followed her in, followed her very closely, not needing his own swipe-card, just catching the door that she had opened before it locked shut again. Leaving no trace of his presence for the police to find.

I could just imagine him, intimidating her, standing at her shoulder, growling and swearing. And once they got to the lab …

Well, once they got in there, he went to the cupboard and got out some latex gloves to threaten her with. She still didn't give in to whatever he wanted, and he wrapped the gloves around her neck and killed her.

To be honest, that last part didn't seem so clear in my mind. Which was strange, because that was the part that we knew the most about. We knew that there were gloves involved, that she died.

But what I was thinking felt … wrong somehow. Well, maybe I just didn't want to imagine her final moments. That was all.

Then after she died, Tony would have taken her phone and thrown it into the lab bin, hoping that it would be disposed of before someone found it and found the incriminating text messages.

Well, I'd found it now. And Bill was on his way. I didn't need to prove that Tony was the murderer. I didn't need to tell Bill anything. He was an intelligent man, and the police were good at working out clues from things like mobile phones. I could just hand it over and wait for Bill to do his job.

I sat back, relaxed and enjoyed my coffee. I could let this go now that I knew who had done the deed. Justice would be served. Everything would come right. Though it was a bit strange that the bin hadn't been emptied in all that time.

30

Bill took the phone, still in its plastic bag and looked at it carefully. He asked me a few times where and how I had found it. But by that stage I was less interested in the story of finding the phone and more interested in getting rid of it. I left the whole thing (as I told him) in his capable hands, and walked briskly back to the chemistry building, hoping that burying my head in my work would distract me enough that I would be able to keep my mouth shut about my conclusions and allow the police to take their time to do the due diligence and to arrest the right person.

But as I walked back to the chemistry building I started to worry. Bill had been very concerned about where I found the phone. Was he starting to suspect me?

I could see how that would work. I mean, the group had all been getting along just fine until I had got there. Then I turn up, and Rebekah is murdered. Then I find Rebekah's phone, in the bin, of all places. It looked a bit dodgy to say the least.

But I knew that I wasn't the murderer. And though I knew it would take longer for them to get through all the details and to fill in the paperwork and break into the phone and all that, than it did for me to so clearly imagine the whole scenario, I was *sure* we had both come to the same conclusion. I *had* to be right about this. I felt a little sick. I hoped that the evidence of the text messages on the phone was enough to point Bill towards Tony and away from me.

I wasn't going to say anything about this to anyone in the chemistry department, but I was so looking forward to the cup of hot chocolate tonight with Martha where I could let everything out. I knew she'd agree with me about what happened and she'd be able stop me worrying that the police would be suspecting me. I mean, how could they suspect me? I didn't do it. I knew that.

All these thoughts and imaginings meant that I didn't notice Tony coming out of Prof Gray's office as I walked past. I nearly bumped right into him.

My face felt hot. I had hoped, really, that I would not see Tony again, or at least only in passing, until I saw him arrested. And here I was, literally running right into him as soon as I got into the building. My first instinct was to run away. But then, that would have looked very strange. And if I acted strangely, he might figure out just what was going on, and he could prepare a defence or run away or something. And if I talked to him now, I could get more evidence to use in case the police really did get the wrong idea about me.

All these thoughts flashed through my head as we mumbled our apologies to each other. Then I noticed the paper he was holding in his hand and I decided that conversation was the most normal-looking thing to do. I would pretend that nothing was odd. That I hadn't just dobbed him in to the police as a killer. I'd just chat. I could do that.

I fell into step with him and we walked together back to the lab.

'Meeting with the big boss?' I asked. He nodded glumly.

'Yeah, he's decided on a weekly check-in for me, now that I'm close to the end. But look at the amount of red pen on this.' He showed me the paper he was carrying. I figured it was a print out of his latest thesis chapter. The page was covered with little notes, underlinings and symbols.

'Red and green pen,' I noted. 'That's Prof's system, isn't it?'

'Red for the things I have to change. And green for the things that he says he's not so attached to – just suggestions, he says.'

I remembered that from working with Prof Gray before. Those suggestions. The sinking feeling in your stomach as you thought that you'd never get the work to the point of completion.

'I don't remember ever being able to change his mind on any of the "suggestions".'

'You've got it.' Tony smiled wryly. 'No, I need to make all the changes. It's going to take me a week.'

'I'm sure you'll be fine.' I said encouragingly.

'It never takes as long as you think. Unless it's experimental work. Then it takes twice as long.'

We both laughed. We were feeling so chummy that I decided to take a risk.

'Tony, I don't want to upset you.' I really didn't. I really hoped he didn't lose his temper again. 'But could you tell me what you meant yesterday – the thing you said about Rebekah?'

'Rebekah …' Tony looked puzzled.

'Yeah, you know, when I had that business card and you said that it was just like what Rebekah did?'

I held my breath. Was I being foolish? I'd just told myself I wasn't going to do anything like this, and here I was all but blurting out my theory that this man right in front of me was a murderer.

'Oh that.' Tony looked a bit ashamed. 'Yeah, I probably shouldn't have said anything about that.'

Damn. Did that mean he wasn't going to tell me anything? I said nothing, hoping he would feel the need to fill the void with an explanation. And he did. He stopped in the corridor and turned to look at me.

'It was …' he said and paused for a long time. Then he started again. 'I had been talking to Rebekah in the lab one time … we were talking about the process it took to get the PhD scholarship. Like, we're both from the same town, you know?'

I nodded, hoping he didn't ask how I knew. He went on.

'We both were awarded the same scholarship. I don't talk about it much, but it's pretty prestigious. You have to write an essay, fill in all these forms, there's even an online test. You go through all this and then there's a big awards ceremony and it's all this fuss.'

'Wow, congratulations. That was a huge achievement.'

'Yeah, thanks.' He smiled briefly. 'I mean, it meant I got to study here, and that's going to do wonders for my career, I know it. So I was pretty happy.'

'So, if you and Rebekah got the same scholarship, well, that means that she's up there too, doesn't it? She's also academically brilliant.'

'It would,' Tony said darkly. 'If she'd done the work.'

'What?'

'Yeah, so we were talking, and she let it slip that her mum had paid someone to help her with the whole application and everything.'

My eyes widened. That's what Sheila had meant about helping Rebekah get out of the house and away from her dad. But then I shook my head. Getting help, that was fine. He didn't need to be so uppity about that. I thought I'd let him know to get off his high horse.

'But surely getting help with these things is normal. I mean, it's all well and good if you can do it all on your own, but if you can't, why not get some tutoring or something? Surely you got people to look over your work too?'

'Yeah, of course I did. And if it had just been help that Rebekah got, that would have been OK. But she told me that this "tutor" had written the whole essay for her. Had even sat the test.'

I looked at him, aghast.

'She told you that?'

'Yeah, she did. She must have been feeling guilty about it or something. But she told me. So yes, I was pretty angry. And to be honest, I'm still angry.'

'I can understand that,' I said. I really could. These scholarships were meant to mean something. And it explained some of why Rebekah wasn't coping with the workload that she had. Here she was, expected to be a super-bright spark in a university full of bright sparks, and she was just a normal student. A student with a mother who had deep pockets. It must have looked like a good idea to Sheila at the time and I could partially understand, but it hadn't really helped Rebekah after all. It had just set her up for failure.

But Tony was not worried about what this did to Rebekah. He was worried about the perceived injustice to himself. He angrily slapped his papers against his leg.

'A dirty trick like that just devalues what I did. I slaved for that scholarship. I worked so hard. And her dear old mum just pays her way into uni. It makes me furious. I nearly told that woman just what I thought of her when I saw her here the other day. But maybe she already knew. Anyway, I'd already said something and it didn't seem to make a lot of difference.'

'You told on her? The uni knows about this? Who did you tell?'

'Yeah ... like she told me what she'd done, and I just ... I was so mad. Then I didn't know who to tell. I thought about telling Prof Gray, but he's so busy, you know? You don't want to disturb him. Like, even today when we were meeting he just rushed his way through the changes and shoved me out the door.

'Then I thought about going to Academic Senate or something. I didn't know which department to tell. Maybe scholarships? I wasn't sure, so in the end I decided to talk with Mike about it. Mike's the 2IC and I thought he'd know what to do. He's been around the traps a bit. So I went and told him.'

'Right. That makes sense I guess. Mike's there for that kind of thing.' I'd seen enough of how the group structure worked to see that Tony's actions made sense.

'So what did Mike say?' I asked.

Tony sighed.

'He told me not to worry about it. That Rebekah would either make it through the PhD or she wouldn't, and there was nothing we could do about things now. And ... I just ... I could see his point of view. But it still makes me angry, you know?' Tony slapped his fist-full of papers against his leg again.

'Sure, I get that. I'd be angry too.'

Angry enough to kill? But the thing was, Tony seemed more resigned than angry. I'd seen him angry, before, in the office. But he got over it quickly, as far as I could tell, and now he was just letting the whole thing pass. And he was talking to me about it too. Would a murderer let out his motive for murder as blatantly as this?

'Anyway, I was getting my own back. I'm going to finish this year, and Rebekah, she was still miles behind. I would have been surprised if she didn't get kicked out for taking too long. So I guess the essay and the test and all the things were good at showing whether you can get through a PhD or not.'

'Well, that's the best form of revenge you can take,' I said, as we swiped our cards at the lab door. Tony smiled and headed through the lab to the office, and I put on the safety glasses and checked on the BET instrument just inside the glass door.

I wondered now what it was that Tony had wanted to talk with Rebekah about. I wished I could ask him, but I couldn't without letting him know that I'd seen the phone. Maybe he wasn't the killer, or maybe he was just a very good actor. I couldn't tell. But now I wasn't nearly as sure that I understood the tale that the text on Rebekah's phone was telling.

31

Later that afternoon I sat at my desk concentrating on putting numbers I had got from the BET instrument into my presentation. It felt so good to fill in some of the holes. I was nearly there.

The seminar and interview were the next day, but as I looked again at my lab diary and my presentation, I couldn't make a final decision on what to present. There was one result that really didn't make any sense and I was wondering whether to include it or not. It was a situation I had been dreading.

I mean, I wanted to make the best impression I could in this seminar, and seminars aren't papers; they don't have to hold all of the information. So it would not be a problem really to just leave that one odd result out. And – I continued to justify to myself – if I had the time I'd go back and repeat the whole experiment from synthesis to analysis to catalysis, and the results might be different the next time. I may have just not left it stirring long enough, right back at the beginning of the process. Or the sample tubes might have got mixed up, despite my careful labelling. There were many innocent reasons why that particular experiment could have gone wrong. I wasn't lying, I was just leaving the outlier out.

But then again, it felt dishonest to say that all of my results were perfect, when one of them so obviously wasn't.

But then, at the same time, did they need to know about a negative result? Journals only publish positives, and the positives really say something. This one result didn't negate all of the others but it might feel like it did if I included it in the presentation. My thoughts went to and fro.

So I was deep in my own personal dilemma when I became aware of the muttering at Rebekah's desk next to me.

'She hasn't done this one either,' came the voice.

'Where are the second-years? I'm never going to get this all finished.'

'Surely there's a list somewhere.'

And a few choice curse words were let loose too.

It was Mike, rooting through Rebekah's papers and muttering to himself. He had a pile of lab books stuck in the crook of his arm, and with his other hand he was trying to sort the general mess in the tiny space available on the desk.

'Can I help you?' I offered. 'There's a bit of space here where you could stack some stuff.'

'It's fine,' came Mike's curt response. 'I'm just having to take over the marking of the labs now that she's gone. It's hard to know where to start. She was so disorganised.'

I could see his frustration. And I figured it was fair. I didn't like talking ill of Rebekah, but if she'd been a bit more organised in life it would have made it easier to take over her jobs after she passed away.

And it looked like there were a few jobs to take over. First-year and second-year undergraduate laboratory report marking, if I heard his mutters correctly. Not to mention any half-finished research. Though that would probably wait for another PhD or honours student to take on. No, it was the laboratory teaching and marking that needed to be sorted out immediately. It looked like she had a fair bit of that to do, and now it had all landed on Mike. I wondered what his regular load was like and how he was going to fit it all in.

Well, this was one thing that wasn't my problem to solve. I didn't need to do any teaching right now. I would teach if I got this job, of course, but the main thing was to get the job.

I turned back to my PowerPoint and decided to leave the dodgy number in. I would do my best not to dwell on it, but I'd not be telling the truth if it wasn't there. I wondered if Martha would be happy to hear me practise again tonight. The seminar and interview were creeping closer. Much closer.

My stomach was starting to roil every time I thought about it. I couldn't wait for tomorrow to be over.

32

'Do I need to open up the church room again?' asked Martha.

'No, I don't need that,' I said. Martha's face dropped so I rushed to reassure her. 'It was really helpful before, thank you so much, but if I could just read through the seminar out loud with my laptop that would be enough.'

Martha was such a beautiful person. Happy to sit through another half hour of boredom just to let me get this talk right. She hardly knew me at all, but here she was, meeting with me for a hot drink every night, and listening to me practise my talk. Not rushing off to the next job. Not running around trying to keep herself busy. I wondered if I'd ever be as content as her. My life at the moment felt much more like I was grasping for things just out of my reach. Would I ever be mature enough to work at a place like this and not worry myself about what other people thought of me? Did I need to stop worrying about getting a university job, and just be content cleaning test tubes, or cleaning toilets for that matter? But was that the best use of my life? Could I be as content as Martha if I worked in an academic position? I didn't know the answer to any of these questions.

Part of me hoped I'd get the job here at Sydney University just so that Martha and I could keep spending time together. She was such a positive influence on me. The mother figure that I had been missing for the past year. I guessed I wouldn't be able to live at St Catherine's forever, I'd have to get my own apartment. But I'd come over for a coffee and catch up regularly, I promised myself.

And if I didn't get the job? I didn't want to think about that. It wasn't helpful to think about that at this stage. I just needed to concentrate on doing my best.

I opened my laptop and placed it where both Martha and I could see it and got started.

'Thank you for that kind introduction. I am very happy to be here and able to share my research on the very important topic of renewable energy.' And on I went.

The talk went smoothly. All the work in the lab and in fine-tuning the presentation had paid off. I was happy with the way the slides flowed into one another. As I came to the end, the tightness in my stomach relaxed. It was going to be OK. At the very least, I was giving it my best shot, and that's all you can do, right? The rest is a lottery.

'Very good, dear.' Martha applauded. I gave a quick curtsey. Then I closed my laptop and we chatted about other things to calm ourselves down.

The best way I could reward Martha for her help was to chat with her about Rebekah-related things.

She was so interested; treating the whole situation like a murder mystery on TV. And as I thought about the day just gone I realised that there were plenty of Rebekah-related stories to tell. It had been a day full of Rebekah, really.

I started by telling Martha about Mike at the desk, picking up all the piles of marking that Rebekah had left unfinished.

'He wasn't happy about it. He was at the desk muttering and moaning, and I could see why. He had this massive pile of marking that he had to do now that she is gone. I don't know how he will get it all done. All that student work. Piles and piles of lab reports.'

'Yes, doing one person's work is hard enough, but doing two … well, I know that when Sam is away and I have to fill in for him, it definitely keeps me on my toes.'

Martha chatted on about her work, the extra things she had to do on occasion, the bits she didn't enjoy. 'Like making sure the bookings are correct. I'm always so scared I'll click on the wrong thing in that blasted computer and book the person in for the week after they were meant to be here, or something like that. It was so much easier when it was all done with a big diary. Then you knew where you were. Pencils worked just fine and you could rub things out if you needed to.'

But I wasn't really listening. I was thinking back to what seemed like years ago, when I'd had that coffee with Rebekah. Hadn't she said something about not teaching, not being able to do the extra work because of her scholarship? I was sure she had. But there she was with the piles and piles of marking. What was she doing with that?

'Anyway Luv, what else happened today? You said that there were a few things that had gone on?'

I shook my head and brought myself back to the present.

'Yes, I found Rebekah's phone.'

'You found her phone? Where?' Martha sat forward, excited by this development.

'It was in the bin, in the lab. I reckon that the killer threw it out there after he'd done the deed.'

'But that was days ago, wouldn't the bin have been emptied by now?' She sat back again in her chair.

'Oh,' I said, surprised. 'I guess ... the bins are usually emptied every day.' I thought about it. 'But maybe the cleaners aren't visiting our lab because of the police investigation.'

'Well that was lucky, Luv. And what were you doing searching through the bins?'

'Oh no,' I laughed. 'I wasn't. But the phone rang. It was so loud.'

I told Martha the story of my lovely white powder spreading all around the balance and she laughed appreciatively.

'Maybe it's time that I buy myself a new phone,' she said. 'I always wait for too long before I replace things.'

I looked at her quizzically. What did my lab mess have to do with her purchasing habits?

'Well,' she explained. 'My old clunker of a phone, if I don't plug it in every single night, the battery is dead by lunchtime the next day. And here's Rebekah's phone lasting so many days, what is it? It's over a week now. And she can still get a phone call? Maybe I need to get a new phone.'

I thought about that, trying to picture the unlock screen again. I hadn't really looked at the battery bar. But there was something else on the unlock screen too. And I couldn't wait to tell Martha about it.

'Martha, you'll be proud of my sleuthing, because I didn't have to unlock the phone or anything, I could just see from the unlock screen that there had been a text to Rebekah, sent on the night she died. And you'll never guess who it was from – it was from Tony.'

'Tony? Who's Tony when he's at home?'

I laughed.

'Tony is the guy who was so upset about the business card.'

'What business card?'

'Look, obviously I've started at the end. Let me try again, starting at the beginning.'

Martha sat back in her chair and folded her hands in her lap and I ran her through all the happenings of my day.

'So you gave the police the phone, knowing it would point them to Tony, but then ...'

'But then Tony and I had that conversation. And you can see why I don't think it was him anymore, can't you?'

'Well … maybe.' Martha didn't look convinced.

'He was so happy to talk with me about everything. He didn't seem to be hiding anything at all.'

'Maybe he thinks that the crisis has passed and that he's not being suspected. So he feels fine to say anything he likes.'

'Well, the police can sort it out anyway. They are the ones who need to worry about this.'

Martha patted me on the shoulder.

'I think you're doing a wonderful job of Miss Marpling.'

'Miss Marpling.' I laughed. 'That's a great job description. If I don't get this job, I'll see if there are any Miss Marpling jobs going. Though I think you're better at it than I am.'

It was Martha's turn to laugh.

'That's 'cause I'm old, Luv. People don't take so much notice of me, and I've been watching people for a very long time. Did anything else happen today?'

'Nope, only that stuff with Mike. But Martha, I've been thinking. Rebekah told me that her scholarship didn't allow her to do any extra teaching. I'm sure that's what she told me. And yet, there she was with all that marking on her desk. So why?'

'She was cheating on her scholarship.' Martha stated it like a fact. I was sure she was getting confused.

'No, she cheated to get her scholarship, according to Tony. She wouldn't cheat on it as well.'

'Once a cheat, always a cheat. Why wouldn't she cheat on the scholarship if she had cheated already?'

'Well … she …' I paused. I really didn't know. Maybe she was cheating on the scholarship. Did she need the extra money? How would I find out?

Martha stood up and took our mugs to the sink.

'Maybe that nice girl would know.'

'The nice girl?' I asked.

'The one who likes Rebekah, you know, it starts with a P.'

'With a P?' I was totally confused now.

'Yes, you told me about her. She was crying. I'm sure her name starts with a P.'

'The one who … oh Yumi?' Yes, that starts with a P. At least we got there in the end.

'Yes, that's her. She might be able to give you some insight into it all.'

'You want me to bring up this painful subject again and accuse Rebekah of cheating in front of her?'

'I'm sure you'll figure it out.' Martha said. Then she yawned widely. 'Well Luv, I think it's time for me to head to bed. You too. You've got a big day tomorrow.'

I wished she hadn't reminded me. I had all but forgotten that the seminar and interview were happening the next day. Now my stomach was churning with adrenaline again. Still, sleep was worth a try.

Martha rinsed out the mugs and I packed up my laptop.

'See you in the morning,' I said.

'Sleep well, Luv,' she responded. 'I'm sure you've got nothing to worry about.'

As I dragged my weary feet up the stairs I thought about all the things I could worry about. The job, the seminar, finding Rebekah's killer. Once again I wished I could be as content as Martha.

33

The next morning, Prof Gray stuck his head around the yellow cupboards.

'Are you ready, Alicia?'

I hit 'Save' one last time on the PowerPoint presentation and closed up my laptop.

'Ready as I'll ever be.'

'I'll take you down and get you set up then,' he said. We were on. This was the moment.

My palms were sweating so that I could hardly hold on to my laptop. I held it to my stomach, trying to calm the butterflies there as well, and to help me calm down I tried to think of other things.

The other things were, of course, all my questions about Rebekah. I thought I'd ask Prof Gray about them. I dived right in.

'Prof, I've noticed over the last few days that Rebekah had been doing a whole lot of marking.'

'Marking?' His tone showed his surprise, but was it surprise about Rebekah marking? Or was it surprise that I'd be asking about Rebekah at this time?

'Yes,' I said. 'The thing is, she told me, you know, before … she said that she didn't have her own students, she wasn't allowed to do any teaching with her scholarship, was she?'

'No,' Prof said slowly. 'She wasn't supposed to be doing any extra work.'

'But Mike went through the stuff on her desk yesterday, and he pulled out a whole lot of first-year books and some second-year reports as well. He was a bit annoyed that she hadn't finished marking them.'

'That is strange. I didn't know anything about that. Mike, you say?'

'Yes, it was Mike looking at the reports.'

'Well, I know he has a lot of students, he has a lot on his plate. Maybe she was helping him out.'

Prof Gray's tone of voice made me think that he had solved the mystery to his own satisfaction, but that answer didn't satisfy me.

'She shouldn't have helped him out though, she didn't have enough time to do her own research.'

'That's probably true. But it's a bit late to worry about that now, isn't it? She should have come to me with her concerns if she had some.'

'Things might have turned out differently if she had.'

'The students know that my door is always open. Anyway there's no point in spreading malicious rumours. I'm sure you have enough sense not to gossip to anyone about this.'

Prof Gray was sounding defensive now. But I wasn't sure that the 'always open' thing held water either. Tony was not willing to go and talk straight to him. Yumi wouldn't even talk to Mike. Maybe that wasn't Prof Gray's fault, but still …

'Speaking of that, did Mike tell you what Tony told him about Rebekah's scholarship?'

Prof stopped walking and turned to face me.

'Sorry, that was a bit complicated, can you say it again?'

'Tony told me that he told Mike that Rebekah cheated on her scholarship. Mike was supposed to tell you. For some reason, Tony didn't want to tell you himself.'

'He should have told me, in fact, if he was serious about it he should have made a submission to academic senate. If he was saying things like that about poor Rebekah he should have been ready to back it up with evidence, and made a formal complaint. You can't have rumours like that going around. I'll thank you not to spread it.'

Prof Gray turned and strode off at a quick pace. The conversation was over. And I may have lost an ally in the team making a decision about my job. Maybe bringing this up right now wasn't such a good idea after all. It hadn't stopped my stomach from bubbling with anxiety, and it hadn't stopped my palms from sweating either. All it had done was make my face burn from embarrassment in addition to all the other problems.

I rushed after Prof Gray, wishing I could go back and take this walk with him again. I'd do things very differently if I could turn back time.

We came to the lecture room door. Now was not the time to be thinking about Rebekah. Now was the time to focus on my seminar, on speaking properly, on answering questions well. Now was the time to earn myself an academic position.

34

As the professor turned on the projectors to warm up and showed me where to plug in my computer, I calmed him down by being extra grateful and keeping the chatter light. I talked about how great it was to have been able to do the extra work for the last couple of weeks, and how close the paper was coming to completion.

There's nothing more calming to an academic than knowing that they are going to be author on another paper. Unless it's learning that they'll be getting more funding. And knowing that, I also implied in my conversation that I'd be applying for funding to support my research if I got this position (which I definitely would) and that I'd love to have Prof Gray on my application.

He thawed out and we were quite chummy by the time we'd worked out the laser pointer and slide changer. We happily presented a united front to the academics who were now coming into the room and finding their seats.

The older professors sat in the front row, not wanting to climb the stairs to the further tiers. Some of them were already retired and had just come in to hear interesting research. Some were white-haired like Prof Gray but were still active in research and teaching. I recognised the Head of School, sitting in the front with the older men, one of the only women in that august group. The next couple of rows were occupied with younger up and coming academics – the associate professors and senior lecturers. Some of the men were dressed in fashionable suits and pointy shoes, some were dressed much more casually in jeans and t-shirts and the women wore tailored shirts and funky jackets over their jeans and sensible shoes.

Behind them sat the lowly post-docs and lecturers. They scattered themselves around the room according to their level of cool (coolest right at the back) or ambition (right behind the senior lecturers). None of this was legislated, but it was the way it always worked out. Human nature is like that.

In a little knot in the back corner were the students from Prof Gray's group. They didn't look as if they belonged at all and their nervous laughter made me think they felt the same way. They were welcome to come and hear me, of course. But they weren't making any decision about my employment prospects in the university. I was encouraged to see them and very grateful that they came. Thinking of how they wouldn't even go to speak to Prof Gray unless invited, I wondered how they felt about the collection of bigwigs in the front row.

Robbie sat with the students, in the same row, but he sat with his legs stretched out over the seat in front and his hands supporting his head so that he could lie back. He looked as if he was on a banana lounge on holidays, not in a lecture theatre listening to a seminar. But I knew that didn't mean that he didn't care. He was someone in the room that I knew had my back.

I really wished that Martha could be there. I would have given a lot to see her friendly smile beaming at me from somewhere in the middle of that audience. I figured I'd just have to imagine her there and give the talk to her. Just block out the important people, and give the talk to someone that I knew loved me.

And then, just as Prof Gray was giving his introduction, the door opened for a latecomer. Mike walked in to the lecture theatre and took a seat pretty much in the centre of the room.

Once I saw him, I couldn't see anyone else. The rest of the room receded into a grey blur. Everything I'd experienced over the past couple of weeks began to make sense and come together.

I stood there like a zombie for long enough that Prof Gray cleared his throat and I remembered where I was.

'Thank you very much, Prof Gray, for your kind introduction,' I said on automatic pilot. 'And thank you all for allowing me to present my research.'

But as I rattled off my carefully rehearsed presentation, as I talked about catalysts, surface area, renewable energies and so on, my mind was racing, thinking on a completely different topic. I suddenly saw that Mike was the connection between all of the questions I had been asking. He was the one who knew about Rebekah's cheating, and he was the one giving her all the extra marking, and it must have been Mike who was threatening her with being 'kicked out'.

I remembered how scared Rebekah was that Mike would see us getting coffee, and how she clammed up and stopped telling me her secret when she saw him in the café the day she died.

I remembered how Yumi had seen him in the office on the night that Rebekah was killed, and how he had 'forgotten' his keys and card so that there was no swipe-card evidence to show he'd been there at all.

I remembered how he'd been in the office when I asked Rob about Tony, and then how Rebekah's mobile phone had shown up so conveniently straight afterwards, with those incriminating texts pointing to Tony as the murderer.

It became clear to me how Mike was getting so much work done. Anything he didn't want to do he was fobbing off on Rebekah. She was doing all his marking, and probably any research tasks that he didn't want to do as well. Formatting references, washing up, literature searching. All the deadly boring stuff. Leaving him free to write huge numbers of papers, and to boost his career.

Did he think that it was going to last forever? Or was he just happy to get that boost for as long as Rebekah could stay in the uni doing her PhD?

And then there I was, poking and prying into Rebekah's private life, and she was prepared to tell me everything. He would have lost his workforce, and his reputation, and probably his position in the uni as well. And he decided to do something about it.

Somehow, probably thanks to Martha and all the practice talks she had willingly sat through, I made it fairly smoothly to the end of the talk, to the acknowledgements slide. And there was Mike's name – I was thanking him for his help with the work. Boy, did those words stick in my throat. But I was so grateful for all the practice that I'd had, and I hoped that the words I'd said actually made sense. In any event, I'd made it to the end.

Now all I had to do was answer questions from the floor.

I'm sure I sounded incredibly vague. I'm not that good at answering seminar questions at the best of times. Give me a couple of hours to think the question through and I'll come up with a great answer, but not straight away. And today it was even harder to get my brain to stay on topic. But eventually it was over. It was time for the morning tea.

35

Corn chips and dip, sausage rolls and tomato sauce, tiny sushi rolls, and some muffins cut into quarters. All laid out on a table just outside the door of the lecture hall. The idea was that I could have casual conversation with the bigwigs, and that they could get to know me a bit. It wasn't formal, but it was important. Part of me wanted to rush off to Detective Bill immediately and tell him everything, but this morning tea was really a part of my interview for the job. I didn't know what to do but in the end I felt I couldn't leave without being rude and jeopardising all my future job prospects. I pulled myself together and chatted and schmoozed. Mike had waited a few days, he could wait a few more.

Out of the corner of my eye, while I was chatting with the Head of School and a lovely old doddery retired professor, I saw Prof Gray take Mike aside. I couldn't hear anything, of course, and couldn't concentrate on them much at all, but the professor was looking very grave, and Mike was waving his hands around and talking very quickly. I saw Prof Gray nod and walk away. And then I caught Mike's eye.

I wished I didn't. I'd never received a look of malice like I saw there. Malice and disgust. My blood ran cold.

And then the big important people moved away and I was surrounded by the group from the lab.

'Great talk,' said Yumi. 'Very interesting.'

'Yeah, you did a good job,' agreed Tony. 'I'm sure you'll get the job.'

'Oh, I'm not,' I admitted. 'I was so nervous.'

'Nah, you were fine,' said Robbie. 'Just as good as any others I've seen.'

I appreciated the back-slapping and support. I wished that the decision was in the hands of this group. But it wasn't. I just had to hope.

'I've still got the interview this afternoon.' I said. This process wasn't over by a long shot.

'Ah, no worries, you'll be fine.' Robbie was so full of confidence for me, and the others were carried away by it too. But I wasn't nearly as confident.

And between now and then I had to find a way to tell the detective what I'd figured out.

36

I had an hour or so before the job interview. I was hoping to slip away to a quiet space by myself and ring Bill, and then take a little time to get my head into the right place to talk to a panel and give a good impression. It should have been easy.

But no.

It seemed that wherever I was, Mike was there too. Not having conversation with me, no, not at all. But just … there. He was in the office when I was there chatting with the rest of the group. He was in the line at the coffee shop when Robbie decided to buy me a pre-interview latte. I thought I'd step out to the hallway and just hang in the corner and phone Bill but there was Mike, just hanging around within earshot. He was just … there.

So I didn't ring Bill. I couldn't figure out how to do it without making it obvious to Mike what I was doing. And I really needed to think about the interview coming up. Why did this all have to happen on the same day?

I checked my black trousers for dust and my white shirt for stains. It was time to face up to the panel of academics and do the actual interview. I pulled myself together and tried to concentrate. I was thinking of answers to questions such as, 'How will this job help you to achieve your long-term career plans?' and 'What experience do you have of attracting funding?' Horrible questions, but I guess they have to ask them.

As I headed to the room for my interview Mike, my new shadow, was there. Following me down the hall at a safe distance. Pretending he was doing something else.

The door to the interview room opened and Prof Gray called my name. I walked through the door and saw the panel of five. Four men and one woman. The woman was the tall and angular Prof Sandison, the Head of School. I knew her because I had met her before in the meeting after Rebekah's death. Not the best thing to be thinking of right now. I knew a couple of others on the panel too; I'd worked with them when I was working here before Mum died. But thinking about Mum's death wasn't going to help either.

Prof Gray tried to put me at my ease, welcoming me and asking me to sit. But he also treated me like he had never seen me before. Like I was a complete stranger. Which was weird considering all the time that we had worked together.

My mind went blank.

This was nothing new. I hate interviews and always struggle with them. So I kind of expected my mind to go blank, my legs to shake, my hands to feel clammy. The questions were asked kindly by all the panel members, but whether we knew each other or not, they treated me like a stranger. No friendly smiles at my attempts at in-jokes, no nods of understanding. Just blank faces asking me hard questions and then not responding to my answers.

Was it because they wanted to treat all applicants fairly? Was it because my answers to their questions were so spectacularly bad? Whatever the reason, I was a bit thrown by their attitudes and I found myself stuttering and stammering more and more as the interview went on.

When the interview was over I nodded and smiled my thanks and left the room hoping to feel a rush of relief as I closed the door behind me. But that was not to be. Because as I closed the door behind me I saw Mike again.

He was loitering outside the interview room and followed me at a discreet distance as I walked with shaking legs back to the office.

'How did it go?' Tony asked as soon as I walked past those yellow cupboards. All the group crowded around me. It was like my interview had engendered a holiday for them all. It was like I had another panel of questions to answer, a panel that for some reason I hadn't expected.

'Oh, I don't know. I hate interviews. It was … they were kind, I guess. But I'm so glad it's over.'

'I'm sure you'll get the job.' Yumi was so kind, and I was grateful for her support, but she was basing her statement on nothing.

Sofia, Sahar, Wei, Yusuf, they were all encouraging. I guess it was exciting for them, being part of the process. I was glad I could offer them excitement, but I didn't feel nearly as confident as they did. Still, I might have felt better about the whole thing if Mike hadn't been standing around on the edges of the conversation, like an annoying mosquito that won't let you relax and sleep.

'You should take the afternoon off now,' Yusuf said. 'You've earned it.'

I glanced over at Mike, standing in the back corner of the office.

'Nah,' I said. 'I'll stay here and pack up. Get my stuff together. Maybe I'll do a little bit of sight-seeing before my plane leaves tomorrow.'

'Do both – pack and sight-see.' Sofia laughed. 'This is Sydney. There is much you can do.'

I laughed it off nervously. I did not want to be alone in Sydney. I did not want my shadow to catch me somewhere alone. I felt much more secure around the group.

So we danced a delicate dance for the rest of the afternoon. Wherever I was, there was Mike, on the edges. I made sure I was always with another member of the group, I was never alone with Mike, but as the afternoon wore on I realised that there was a flaw in my plan.

Slowly the group members went home. One by one they left, giving me a cheery, 'goodbye, and good luck' or a big hug and a promise to come down to Tassie to visit. I was packing my desk, packing my samples away in the lab again, and saying my goodbyes. Robbie left, and Wei, Yusuf and Sofia walked down the stairs together. Yumi packed her Hello Kitty laptop away and gave me a hug with tears in her eyes, and made her way through the lab and away. And I suddenly realised that if I didn't leave soon, I'd be in the lab alone with Mike, and that would be even worse than being outside with him.

So when Sahar picked up her handbag, the last in the office except for Mike and myself, I threw the final bits and pieces into my backpack and stood up to leave with her.

We walked through the lab, placing our safety glasses on the table beside the door. But Sahar didn't leave the way I was expecting her to. Instead, she opened the lab door and let someone in. I realised that she and her friend were going to take the fire escape exit, the quick way, rather than walking through the building to leave.

As they wandered through the lab chatting in Persian I had a decision to make. Should I go out with them, down the fire escape and into the side alley, or should I instead leave through the building. Which would be safer? Not many people were around either way, but in the end I decided that the brightly lit halls of the chemistry building would be a better choice.

So I waved goodbye to Sahar, and retraced my

steps through the lab and down the inside stairs. About halfway down I heard the lab door open behind me.

I could see through the windows that it was dark outside. I had put off leaving for too long. It wasn't quite after hours yet; the sign out book didn't need to be used. But it was Friday afternoon. The building was all but deserted. Offices locked. Labs empty and lights turned off.

If I had been nervous before the interview I was a wreck now. I could feel trickles of sweat running down my back, my stomach was tight, my breath coming in short gasps. I wondered if I could run all the way to St Catherine's. Would the adrenaline I was feeling give me super-human strength or ability? I was pretty sure I wouldn't be that lucky.

I was sure that the footsteps behind me were Mike's but I forced myself not to turn and look. And then I didn't have to look, because he was right there at my shoulder.

'You think you're so smart.' His voice was quiet and menacing. 'You've worked it all out, haven't you? Why couldn't you just mind your own business?'

I stopped and turned to face him.

'What? What have I worked out?' I asked, trying to make my voice sound calm and pleasant.

'Nah, you won't get me that easily,' he said. 'How about you hand over your phone? I don't want you recording anything that would get me into trouble.'

He clicked his fingers impatiently. 'Come on. Don't try to do anything brave or stupid.'

I wasn't brave. I was just about to fall down, my legs felt so weak. I searched in my bag and handed over my phone. I almost laughed. I hadn't thought of anything so smart as recording a confession. All I wanted to do was get away. And it looked like I wouldn't.

'What are you going to do?' I asked raising my voice just in case there was someone around in one of the nearby offices. 'Are you going to try to kill me too? I'm not allergic to latex, you know.'

'No, of course you aren't. But there are many things that can go wrong in a lab. I'm sure we can work something out.' He grabbed my arm and started walking me back to the stairs. His grip felt like a metal pincer. I almost let out a scream for help, but as he dragged me back up the stairs he started talking. It was probably very foolish, but my curiosity got the better of me, and though I struggled, I also listened to his story.

'I didn't mean to hurt her, you know. Well not to kill her, anyway. She was just getting a bit too big for her boots. I needed to shut her up.'

'If you didn't mean to hurt her, then that's good,' I said. 'You could plead manslaughter. You could …'

'Lose everything,' he said flatly. 'I'll lose it all. My career, my life, my freedom. Rebekah, she was a mistake. I was only trying to keep her doing that extra work for me. But if I let you blab now, I'll lose it all. Not just my extra time, but everything. I can't let that happen. You are much more of a threat than Rebekah ever was.'

We approached the glass lab door.

'Now, give me your swipe-card,' he said.

'We could use yours.' My voice came out as a nervous squeak.

'No. I'm not here. There will be no evidence of me being here.'

I fumbled in my bag.

'Get on with it,' he growled.

I wasn't trying to take my time. I was just so scared now that my fingers felt like blocks of wood. I couldn't figure anything out.

'Oh come on,' he said impatiently. 'I should have put the gloves on before I came out. Even if it went wrong last time.'

'What?' I said, still fumbling.

'Oh you might as well know,' he sighed. 'That was the mistake. I put the gloves on, you know, to hide the evidence. But there she was, all allergic. More than I thought she would be.'

My fingers finally found the keychain and swipe-card in the bottom of my bag. But I didn't let Mike know. Instead I encouraged him to keep talking.

'So, you wore some latex gloves so that your fingerprints wouldn't be noticed when you threatened Rebekah.' I fumbled some more as I forced my wooden fingers to pull the keys into the right configuration. 'And then she had that allergic reaction. What did you do? Try to strangle her?'

'No, of course not,' he said in a very matter of fact tone that chilled me through. 'I held her by the shoulder, and put my hand over her mouth. I didn't trust Yumi's headphones to block all the noise out if she started to scream.'

'But ... why latex gloves? You had to go to the cupboard for them.'

'Well, nitrile wouldn't have been threatening, would it? Latex was my weapon. She was just a little more highly allergic than I thought. And maybe having a hand on her mouth was just a bit too far.' Mike was musing now. Thinking it through. Solving it like a research problem.

'But that's not going to work for you, is it?' He asked. 'I'm going to have to think of something else. HF, do you think? Or maybe some form of cyanide? I'm glad you said the interview wasn't great, it will be easier to convince people of suicide now.'

I started to shake. I wondered if I'd be able to scream loudly enough to get some help from the people around. I wondered if anyone in this big city would care that I was about to be murdered.

I wrapped my fingers around the keys and made a fist with a key sticking out. Then as I pulled my hand out of the bag I jabbed at Mike's face and at the same time I screamed as loudly as I could.

'Help!'

Mike dodged, I didn't manage to scratch him, but the main thing was that he let me go. I turned to run again and ran straight into someone as solid as a wall.

'Whoa there, hold on,' said a familiar voice. It was Bill. I had never been so glad to see a detective in my life. And there had been moments before.

I heard Mike run past us and thought he'd get away, but almost immediately his footsteps stopped.

Bill and I both turned to see what was going on. There was Mike, his shoulders slumped, his whole body a picture of disgrace. I looked past him to see Prof Gray standing in the hallway, his expression one of deep disappointment and disdain. I realised that whatever Mike went through now, this would be the moment when he knew it was all over. There was no way that his life goals and dreams could come to pass now. Professor Geoffrey Gray, Mike's mentor, knew. Knew what Mike had done. Knew about Mike's cheating, his blackmail, and his murderous nature. There was no one who would give Mike a job now. No one to help him on his way to professorship. He was done.

Bill walked over to Mike. And while Mike stood there passively and silently, offering no resistance, he handcuffed him and read him his rights.

It was finally over. All the nervous energy drained out of me and I sank to the ground.

37

I didn't get back to St Catherine's until very late that night.

There was a lot of waiting. Waiting for uniformed police to come to the chemistry building and take Mike away. Waiting for Bill to interview Mike. Writing my statement (that took a long time, there was a lot to write). I have to tell you that everything they say about police station coffee is true, it was no wonder that Bill always wanted to meet in the café over from the chemistry building.

But when I did get back to St Catherine's, dropped off in a police car, Martha was there waiting for me. She looked dreadful. She gave me a massive hug.

'I was so worried. I was about to ring the police to report you missing.'

I shivered. I realised just how important that might have been. If Bill hadn't turned up, then Martha's phone call to the police might just have been the thing that got them looking. Got them finding me, dead, in the lab. Tears started to roll down my cheeks.

Martha took charge.

'Come on in, Luv. Come and have a hot chocolate. And tell Martha all about it.'

I sniffed and wiped my face.

'It's late, Martha, I can't keep you up longer tonight.'

'And you think I'll sleep without some explanation about what's happened? No, come and tell me all about it. I need to know.'

That made me laugh, despite the tears. But we went inside.

This time, Martha sat me on a window seat in the dining room. She found a blanket from somewhere and wrapped me in it. And then she disappeared into the kitchen for a few minutes and came out with steaming cups of hot chocolate.

'I broke out the marshmallows,' she said. 'It looks like you could do with some sugar as well.'

I took a sip. The sugar did help, it was true. I'd never had a more comforting hot drink in my life.

And then I told her the story. It was a different version of the story than that in my police report – there was a lot more of the emotion, and a lot more of the conjecture.

'So it was Mike, all the time. We didn't even think of him.'

'No, it didn't become clear until I started telling Prof Gray. But then it was super clear.'

'And it was clear to Mike then too, that he had to get rid of you?'

That made me shudder.

'I don't know. He might have already decided I needed looking after. But I'm glad I did tell Prof

Gray. You see, after he heard my story he went to Mike and asked him a few hard questions. Mike did a lot of quick talking, but his answers made Prof Gray more suspicious than my accusations had in the first place. He looked into things a bit himself, and then he called the police.'

'Smart man.'

'I guess so.' I smiled. 'He is a professor after all.'

'I'm glad he used his brains for more than just science.'

'Me too. Anyway, the police couldn't really act on that. Not even a professor's word is enough for them to arrest someone. They need evidence. But it did give them enough cause to go and search Mike's house.'

'Ooooh really?' Martha's eyes were wide with excitement.

'Yes. And when they searched they found Rebekah's epipen. It had her name on it. I think they found it in the rubbish.'

'Her epipen?'

'The pen with adrenaline that she was supposed to use to treat herself when she had an allergic reaction. If she'd had that pen with her when Mike had threatened her, she might have lived. And she told me that she kept it in her desk drawer. So she should have had it there.'

'And then Bill went to the uni to find you?'

'Well, actually, Bill and Prof Gray were both coming up to find Mike and see what he had to say for himself. Or if he wasn't there, they were going to have a look through his desk. Prof Gray used his swipe-card to let Bill in the front door, and the two of them were on their way to the lab so that Prof Gray could let Bill in there too. And that's where they found us.' My voice cracked as I remembered again just how scared I was.

Martha comfortingly patted my arm, and made sure that I was properly tucked up in the blanket. Then she started musing again.

'So that pen, that adrenalin pen being found at Mike's place, that means, on the night that Mike "accidentally" gave Rebekah an allergic reaction, he had the chance to fix it?'

I nodded.

'That's the thing. He could have treated her. He could have saved her life. He had the pen. But he didn't. So Bill told me that he thinks this was actually premeditated. It was planned. It was murder, dressed up to look like an accident.'

'But Mike told you it was an accident.'

'I think he was trying to convince himself. But the evidence speaks differently. Anyway, it's up to a jury now I guess. The main thing is that he's locked away.'

'Yes, dear. That's a very good thing.' Martha smiled and nodded gently. Then she sat up and looked questioningly at me. 'And how did the interview go, Luv? And the seminar? How do you feel about that?'

This time I laughed loudly. I had almost forgotten that those important things had happened.

'Oh Martha, I honestly don't know. My head was so full of Mike and murder, I think I probably messed the interview up entirely. I wasn't exactly at my best today. Not with that man hanging around threateningly, not with the murder plot coming together in my head. I think I've stuffed it.'

She sat back in her chair.

'Well, you've done the most important thing, anyway. We'll leave the rest up to God.'

'I guess we will.' I yawned hugely. 'Can I go to bed now?' I asked plaintively.

'Of course, Luv. Go to bed. Sleep well. And sleep in. I can keep breakfast for you if you don't make it down on time.'

She gathered the cups and I pulled the blanket around myself and dragged my tired feet up the stairs to my bedroom. I didn't even bother to get changed, I just took my shoes off and fell into bed and slept a deep and dreamless sleep.

38

'And that was it, really.' I said to Jan and Nate. 'That was the end of the story. I caught the plane this morning and came home. So you see, it was sort of my fault.'

'It was not!' Jan shook her head firmly.

'No, it wasn't your fault.' Nate's tone was more measured, but his meaning was the same. 'Mike always had a choice and he was doing the wrong thing from the start. I guess you'll have to go back up to testify in court.'

'You never know, I might have to go back up because I have a job there.'

'Yes, there's always that,' Jan agreed. 'I wonder how the group members have coped with it all?'

'I reckon Yumi would have cried again. Robbie will be wondering who will take Mike's place. Tony will say that he always suspected Mike of doing something like that. Sophia won't even care, I reckon. Wei will have had the most exciting honours year ever. Nothing will ever compare to it.'

'Spoiled for the ordinary,' said Nate.

I yawned, my mouth opening so wide it was impossible to hide.

'You must be exhausted.' Jan was all concern. 'And we've kept you up listening to your story.'

'No, no. It was good to debrief. But I feel like I could sleep for weeks now.'

'Your bed is all ready for you. We'll run you home and leave you to it.'

I hadn't heard any sweeter words in the last two weeks and I was sure I wouldn't hear anything sweeter for some time to come. My own bed.

39

Two weeks later, on a Monday afternoon, I came back from a walk on the beach to find that two emails had appeared in my inbox.

The first began with, 'We regret to inform you …'

Well, that was to be expected when you are trying to catch a killer while performing a job interview and seminar. I mean, my head had been in a completely different space to what it should have been. I reckon if I could watch a video of that seminar it would look like I was on drugs or something.

The second email was from Prof Gray.

Dear Alicia,

I know that you didn't get the position you wanted. However, as you well know, I now find myself without a 2IC for my group. I have received permission from the school to offer you a one-year postdoctoral contract, taking over Mike's position.

I am sure you will do a wonderful job of helping me manage my group. And I am sure you will not have any of the issues that Mike seems to have been plagued with.

I hope that you will agree to join us. Please let me know as soon as possible.

Best, Geoffrey Gray.

So I didn't get *the* job, but I did get *a* job. Now I just needed to decide whether it was right, whether it was time to get back into the slog of writing and research.

Maybe I'd give it a go for one year and then see what happened next. I just hoped that I wouldn't be involved in any more murders. I could do without that for a while. Probably for the rest of my life.

The End

* * *

I hope you enjoyed Alicia's adventure. It would be a kindness if you would leave a review on your favourite vendor website.

Come over to www.rjamos.com and sign up to my newsletter to hear all my news and to find out when the next book is coming out. I'd love to see you there!

* * *

Other books by R. J. Amos

Deadly Misconduct (Book 1 in the Deadly Miss series)
Deadly Misdirection (Book 2 in the Deadly Miss series)

Small Town Trouble
Challenge Accepted – A 30-day Short Story Project
The Universe is a Small Place

Find out more at rjamos.com